TERRORISTS IN THE HEARTLAND

A Novel by

John W. Gemmer

CCB Publishing
British Columbia, Canada

Terrorists in the Heartland: A Novel

Copyright ©2019 by John W. Gemmer
ISBN-13   978-1-77143-397-6
First Edition

Library and Archives Canada Cataloguing in Publication
Title: Terrorists in the heartland / a novel by John W. Gemmer.
Names: Gemmer, John W., 1948- author.
Identifiers: Canadiana (print) 20190137282 | Canadiana (ebook) 2019013741X |
ISBN 9781771433976 (softcover) | ISBN 9781771433983 (PDF)
Classification: LCC PS3607.E55 T47 2019 | DDC 813/.6—dc23

Cover artwork: Cornfield in the heartland of America | ShutterStock.com

Publisher: CCB Publishing
British Columbia, Canada
www.ccbpublishing.com

Dedication

I am dedicating this book to the first responders who died as a result of the 9/11 attacks in the United States and to their families.

Acknowledgements

Thanks to Kevin Sheets and Hope Heritz for their help and encouragement.

Special thanks to Tammy Landers-Dressler, my editor, Jeff Rasley, a consultant, and Paul Rabinovitch, my publisher, CCB Publishing, British Columbia, Canada.

Books by John W. Gemmer

The Last Assignment

Harsh Consequences

Terrorists in the Heartland

Prologue

It was 1:30 a.m. on Sunday, October 6, 1974, in the suburbs of Sanaa, Yemen. A rusty and faded white utility van moved slowly along the main highway leading out of town. The nondescript looking vehicle was hardly noticeable apart from its headlights that were visible through the on-going sand storm that was raging in Sanaa. A few seconds later, the vehicle turned left off the main highway onto a smaller paved road and then right again onto a narrow dirt road. The dirt road was adjacent to a six-foot high concrete block wall that surrounded the rear of the United States Embassy compound. The concrete wall had been constructed with electrified barbed wire at the top.

The van stopped near the middle of the wall, and its rear door opened slowly. A man got out and retrieved a ladder from the roof. He grabbed a large piece of carpet with a rubber backing, from inside the van, and threw it over the wall. Then, he placed the ladder against the concrete wall, and four people emerged from inside the van and quickly climbed over. Once the team had gotten over the wall, the driver drove the vehicle into an alleyway, across the road, and waited.

Once inside the compound, the team made their way into the loosely guarded back lot of the annex building that had been recently constructed on the Embassy grounds. The waning early morning moon, along with several broken flood lights, made it possible for the small, Islamic extremist team to infiltrate the compound easily. Due to a shortage of computer components, the team had been informed that the security system in the new building was not going to be completed until later in the week. The information about the annex's vulnerability was the main reason the team leader had chosen to proceed with the operation, despite very little preparation. The team consisted of a trained operative leader and two armed body guards for security. At the last minute, the leader added a young and spirited Yemeni female trainee to be placed as a lookout.

She was motivated to get involved in the Islamic extremist movement, due to the fact that her father and older brother had been killed by a United States ship. The ship had rammed their family's fishing vessel, leaving no survivors. Their vessel had literally been run over by this huge oil freighter, the type that is commonly seen going through the Suez Canal. Their cargo consisted of millions of barrels of crude oil on its way to American refineries. She was saddened and believed it was her duty to avenge their deaths, in spite of the fact that she was only five feet tall, extremely shy, naïve, and inexperienced.

Sanaa was extremely windy that morning. The blinding sand had allowed the team to swiftly cross the yard and arrive at the entry door to the annex, without encountering a security detail. The extremist team members were tasked to obtain several classified files in the annex building pertaining to United States counter-terrorism activity in Yemen. The documents were located inside a secure filing cabinet, and the leader believed the contents, if acquired, would be very useful for future terrorist planning. The team had been provided with the location of the files, along with duplicate keys for the annex door and the filing cabinet. They had watched the Embassy for a week in order to determine the exact schedule followed by the guards for patrolling that particular building.

At 1:40 a.m. the team entered the building. The female team member was stationed near the front door, while the others headed upstairs. Several minutes later, she saw a beam of light outside coming towards the building. She heard the front door being unlocked and saw the door open. She watched nervously as a military sentry unexpectedly entered the building. The sentry failed to notice her presence behind him, but quickly turned upon hearing the sound of her breathing. As the sentry turned and reached for his weapon, the woman grabbed a large paperweight from a nearby desk and used it to knock the unsuspecting guard unconscious. Almost immediately, he collapsed on the floor, and unbeknownst to her, died instantly from the blunt force trauma to his face. The startled and scared Yemeni woman swiftly climbed the stairs to the second floor, in order to notify the others about what had just transpired. They were not far from her location and quickly accompanied her downstairs, to where the guard remained.

After the assault, a pool of blood had already begun to form underneath the man's forehead. When the other team members arrived, they found the guard lying on the floor, face down, and deceased. The young woman had quickly responded on behalf of the team. She had been forced to protect herself. The operation, although dangerous, was not expected to be perilous. In fact, it was supposed to have been a moderately complicated, in and out, fifteen minute operation. Unfortunately, the guard arrived for some unknown reason thirty minutes too early and paid the ultimate price for his untimely appearance. The killing was necessary to safeguard the woman and her other team members, who would have been undoubtedly captured, thrown into prison, interrogated, tortured, and possibly executed for espionage. The greatly troubled woman was assured that once the team cleaned up the mess, and disposed of the body, the event would be over and forgotten.

The distressed young woman's only job had been to watch the front door and alert the others to any approaching trouble outside. Afterwards, because of her brave response, she was praised by the team leader and instructed to continue working at the Embassy, as though nothing had happened.

Even though the killing had transpired twenty-five plus years earlier, sometimes late at night the guard's death still continues to haunt her. She would never forget the wrenching look on his face after the paperweight first impacted his nose. At the time, the event caused her a lot of distress. It had been her first and only killing, to date. Many soldiers will tell you, your first kill will always be remembered and possibly troubling.

At the time, she did what any disciplined, well-trained warrior would have done to survive. After the team had cleaned up the floor, removed the body from the building, lifted it over the wall, and left the compound, almost everyone seemed relieved. Thirty minutes later, the team was more than several miles outside of Sanaa and had picked a remote location where they buried the body in a shallow grave. The Yemeni woman recalled how the other team members, more hardened than she, had seemingly returned to their homes, almost unscathed, as if nothing had happened. However, she was still extremely troubled. The operation had not been a success, because they had been forced to leave abruptly without obtaining any of the documents. Nonetheless, their entry had gone undetected, regardless of the guard's mysterious disappearance. The killing seemed to be just another necessary act of violence, justifiable within the team's extremist parameters, and the continuation of the war that had begun years earlier.

Prior to the September 11, 2001, attacks on the Twin Towers, the United States Embassy bombing in Beirut, Lebanon, on April 18, 1983, killing 63 and injuring 120, was one of the first major terrorist activities waged against the United States government. The former female operative continued to remind herself of the constant spilling of Muslim and non-Muslim blood that had started in the early 1970's and continued with the 9/11 attacks. Following the 9/11 attacks, she became curious to learn about all the Islamic extremist attacks that had occurred worldwide since the 1970's. She was interested in how much human carnage those attacks had caused. To her surprise and appreciation, she discovered that all those attacks combined were responsible for 6,085 deaths and 21,514 injuries. The lengthy number of terrorist attacks that had occurred also amazed her, along with their impressive results.

As she contemplated the accomplishments of the various groups associated with the Islamic extremist organizations, a stark truth occurred to her. She had been proud to be one of the many warriors involved in carrying out the on-going successful campaign of Jihad against the West. Over the years, she had allowed her conscience to occasionally bother her. However, at the time, she always found ways to justify her actions. Going forward, she continued to put as much distance as possible between the memories of her past and the hopes for her future.

Nevertheless, years later, she would experience another disturbing and infuriating event that once again motivated her to help the Islamic extremists. But, this time her motivation would be about acquiring money for herself, instead of just seeking revenge against the West.

TERRORISTS
IN THE
HEARTLAND

Chapter 1

At 6:00 a.m., Frank Giordano's alarm clock began its normal, yet annoying, chime. After several seconds, he reached over, shut it off, and briefly went back to sleep. Fifteen minutes later, the noise from a backfiring vehicle in the neighborhood, startled and awakened him. Reluctantly, he decided it was time to get up. The aroma of fresh Columbian coffee had already permeated into the bedroom. Frank was thankful that his wife, Marie, had gotten up early to make coffee for them.

He ambled into the bathroom, showered, brushed his teeth, and shaved. Frank admired himself in the mirror as he splashed a small amount of Old Spice aftershave on his face. He looked and felt pretty good, in spite of attaining the age of 50. His well-proportioned physique was that of a younger man. He also knew that his olive skin, manly looking face, and brown bedroom eyes were deemed appealing by Marie, and some of the other attractive neighborhood women.

Today was September 11, 2002, exactly one year from the day that had changed the American way of life forever and had changed Frank's life significantly too. He thought of that fact, as he dressed for work and rushed downstairs. "The coffee smells really inviting this morning," he commented to Marie, as he hastily entered the kitchen, grabbed a large insulated container full of coffee, a chocolate donut, kissed her good-bye, and rushed out the back door for work. "I don't want to be late again," he said. "I have enough problems; I don't need any more. Have a good day, honey."

"You have a good day too. I'll see you tonight," she said. "Love you too," she proclaimed quietly, knowing that he had not heard much of what she had said anyway. Marie understood and forgave him for his indiscretions, knowing full well that Frank occasionally took her for granted. She knew that he loved her, but at times, he allowed his job to take precedence over her.

Frank had worked his way up the FBI chain of command and had attained a distinguished and responsible position in the counter-terrorism division of the Bureau. He was stationed in Washington, D.C. prior to the attacks, but afterwards was reassigned to a new duty station in Michigan. Prior to the transfer, he had been removed as a special agent in the counter-terrorism division. Unfortunately, the reassignment and demotion caused a reduction in his salary, but it had not seriously affected his lifestyle. The cost of living in the Washington, D.C., area was far more expensive than in Michigan. More importantly though, Frank's pride and self-worth had been shattered, which had more of an effect on him than his loss of pay.

On the drive to his downtown office in Grand Rapids, Michigan, Frank thought about the reports that he had prepared after the al-Qaeda attacks. They were so familiar to him he could almost recite the events and details by memory. The world would never forget September 11, 2001, and neither would Giordano. His detailed reports included the typical "cover your butt" commentary, which was always necessary when communicating to a large bureaucracy, like the United States Federal Bureau of Investigations.

After the attacks, The Central Intelligence Agency had been primarily blamed by The White House for not informing President George W. Bush of the warnings, trying to shield the new administration from public criticism and responsibility. However, Frank had heard from a reliable CIA source, the warning of strikes being imminent had been given to President Bush in May 2001. Also, it was rumored an Arab CIA operative, close to Osama bin Laden, had told the Agency that bin Laden planned to use suicide bombers on airplanes to destroy his targets.

At 8:46 a.m., on that fateful Tuesday morning of September 11, 2001, Frank remembered watching the hijacked American Airlines Boeing 767 jetliner slice into the 80th floor of the North Tower at the World Trade Center. The airplane had been commandeered by five militants, affiliated with the Islamic extremist group, known as al-Qaeda. A second hijacked airplane, piloted by yet another five al-Qaeda militants, crashed into the South Tower about seventeen minutes later. Both towers were heavily damaged, and both ultimately collapsed. He remembered thinking how surreal it was as he watched the live NBC News Special Report, in his Naples, Florida, hotel room, showing the second plane hitting the South Tower in real time.

At 9:37 a.m., a third hijacked airliner, controlled by five more al-Qaeda militants, crashed into the Pentagon in Arlington, Virginia. A fourth hijacked jet airplane crashed at 10:03 a.m. in a remote field in Shanksville, Pennsylvania, killing all aboard. In the moments before the Shanksville crash, the four al-Qaeda extremists onboard were overrun by the passengers on the flight. It was theorized the plane's final destination would have been The White House, Camp David, The Capital complex, or perhaps an East Coast nuclear facility.

He learned a total of 2,996 people died that day as a result of the attacks. In New York City alone, there were 2,761 deaths, including 400 police officers and firefighters, and 155 airline passengers. At the Pentagon in Virginia there were 190 deaths, of which 125 were military personnel and civilian and 65 were airline passengers. There were 45 passenger deaths in the crash that occurred in Pennsylvania. In addition, Giordano was aware that more than 6,000 people had been injured in the attacks on the World Trade Center.

Eventually, over the next five days, the world would learn that nineteen al-Qaeda militants, mostly from Saudi Arabia and several other Arab nations, were responsible for the attacks. They had hijacked four United States passenger jet airplanes intending to carry out suicide missions against important predetermined targets in the

New York City and Washington, D.C., areas. Ultimately, three out of the four attacks were successful.

After reading a classified CIA report, Frank learned that Osama bin Laden and Ayman al-Zawahiri, bin Laden's right-hand man, were thought to be the chief architects of the September 11 attacks.

Al-Zawahiri was an Egyptian born physician and bin Laden's personal doctor before the inception of al-Qaeda. He is said to have been a bookworm as an adolescent. He excelled at his studies and had been described by knowledgeable Arabs as being brilliant. The pair met sometime in the 1980's after al-Zawahiri had already begun his own Islamic Jihadist group. Ultimately, this friendship lead bin Laden's al-Qaeda and al-Zawahiri's Egyptian Islamic Jihad to unite into one destructive organization.

As Giordano watched the news coverage on September 11, he immediately understood that America was under attack. He wondered if the attacks had been perpetrated by the terrorist group known as al-Qaeda.

Shortly thereafter, on October 7, 2001, Operation Enduring Freedom was launched by President George W. Bush. The operation was an American led international effort, orchestrated by the United States President and his advisors, to oust the Taliban in Afghanistan and to destroy Osama bin Laden's al-Qaeda network. The military operation was very successful, but Osama bin Laden and some of his upper echelon militants had evaded capture, despite the efforts of American and International forces. It was thought that bin Laden had relocated somewhere in the mountains of Afghanistan.

Frank had been on an overdue family vacation with Marie when September 11 occurred. Almost immediately, he was summoned to return to the FBI headquarters in Washington, D.C. The newly appointed FBI Director, Robert S. Mueller III, called for a total effort by the Bureau to help with the investigation. That meant all hands on-deck in the FBI headquarters offices. Giordano was one of the lead special agents in the Bureau's Counterterrorism Division. His superiors expected him to help piece together the events surrounding the attacks.

CIA Director, George J. Tenet, had been placed on the hot seat by Bush surrogates blaming him and the Agency for not informing President Bush of possible future attacks. The Democrats and even some Republicans were applying political pressure on the new president, and as a result, there was a lot of push back from The White House staff. Giordano knew at the time there would be sacrifices and scapegoats used to protect the people at the top. However, Frank had no idea that he was about to become one of those scapegoats.

The FBI was able to avert most of the blame, because they had made a major arrest of an al-Qaeda terrorist in Minnesota prior to the September 11 attacks, which turned out to be a very important development. However, the arrest had not been immediately communicated to the upper echelon at the Bureau, at least, that is what the upper echelon thought, but Giordano thought he knew differently.

The case involved the arrest of Zacarias Moussaoui, a

French citizen of Moroccan decent, by FBI agents. Moussaoui was an al-Qaeda terrorist wanting to train on a 747-flight simulator, in spite of the fact that he was not a pilot. Ultimately, it was determined, Moussaoui was supposed to have been the fifth hijacker on flight 93 that had crashed in Pennsylvania. Also, it was learned after the attacks, that some of the terrorists had been living in the United States on expired visas and had taken flying lessons at American flight schools. This information had somehow been missed by the Bureau and several other Federal agencies. Giordano knew heads were going to roll because of those errors.

Frank had been assigned to follow up on the Moussaoui investigation after the original case investigator left the Bureau for a lucrative political appointment in the Justice Department. The original agent assured Frank that he had reported the complete details of the case up the chain of command to the proper authorities. Once Giordano was told the report had never been received by his superiors, he immediately forwarded them a copy. Giordano believed that the agent's report had somehow been lost in the transition. Unfortunately, Giordano was blamed for the failure to communicate the arrest of Moussaoui, and to report its significance in the proper manner and on time.

Several months later, he was transferred from the headquarters office and reassigned to a small regional office in Southwest Michigan, because of the incident. For the last ten months, Giordano has been stuck there handling trivial crimes instead of major cases involving terrorism. He was angered and somewhat bitter by his obvious demotion.

Occasionally, Frank would be called upon, as a last resort, to assist in the investigation of cases within the jurisdiction of the Grand Rapids, Michigan, office. Most of these cases were minor involving surveillance activities on low level organized criminals. Also, he had done some surveillance work involving Aryan, African American, and Latino biker gang members in the Southwest Michigan town of Benton Harbor. For the most part, Frank felt he was only being utilized to cover for other agents when they were either on extended leave for illness or on vacation.

Giordano and his wife Marie were currently residing in the community of Wyoming, a suburb of Grand Rapids. He liked the change of scenery, and his co-workers, but unfortunately, his alleged botch had followed him from Washington, D.C. Tom Murrell, the special agent in charge of the Grand Rapids office, appreciated Frank's length of service and experience but not his reputation. Any perceived failure by an FBI agent in regards to the September 11, 2001, investigation was not looked upon favorably, no matter what the circumstances.

Frank had considered leaving the FBI but decided against it because of the sizable government pension he had accumulated. Besides, he hoped to someday rebuild his prior reputation as being a responsible, qualified, and capable agent. Being stationed in Grand Rapids made him wonder just how long that might take.

Chapter 2

Wednesday morning, ten minutes after Giordano had left for work, he was stuck in the usual early morning traffic jam. He waited patiently in the endless line of vehicles, barely moving towards the downtown exits. The short commute took nearly twenty minutes, but it gave Frank quiet time to think. This morning, he had been thinking about the frightening effects the September 11 attacks had on the country, the substantial devastation, and loss of life everyone in the country felt. Turning onto the Cherry Street exit, he reminded himself once again, as he had done countless times before, how those attacks had been detrimental for him as well.

By mid-morning, Frank was ready to go home. He gazed out his office window and thought to himself, *thank God, another day almost half over.* It had been just as boring and uneventful as the previous workday. He was tiring of the same old routine. After all, even the least uneventful work day in Washington, D.C., had been more rewarding and challenging than what was considered to be a busy day in Grand Rapids.

He could never imagine how a dedicated and qualified agent, like himself, could have ended up in this predicament. His religious background had prepared him for life not for the political realities of working for a bureaucratic organization, like the Federal Government. He was innocent of the Bureau's charges, but because of politics, and he believed because of a dishonest agent, he was being used to protect the higher ups.

Lately, he found himself thinking about his life, his family, and other challenges he may have faced, had he never become an FBI agent. He wondered what his life would have been like had he followed in his father's footsteps and gone into law enforcement. How would he have handled dealing with drug dealers and addicts? Maybe he would have enjoyed chasing down murder suspects to see that they were punished for their crimes.

In 1952, Frank was born to Ernesto and Fantasia Giordano. His mother was a beautiful Italian woman, very bright, and positively charming. Ernesto married Fantasia three months after they had met. They immediately proceeded to start a family and within five years, were blessed with four children.

Fantasia was responsible for naming Frank, Francis Albert Giordano, after New Jersey's favorite son, Francis Albert Sinatra. Over the years, he had listened to his mother tell of how captivated she had been by the famous Italian singer from Hoboken, as were most of the other Italian women in the neighborhood. More than once, she had disclosed to him her dream that someday, no matter his chosen profession, he would become as famous as Sinatra.

His father, Ernesto Giordano, a former Morristown police officer, walked a beat for thirty-plus years before he retired from the police department. Ernesto was a second-generation Italian American. He and all his children were born, raised, and schooled in the Catholic parish of St. Jude's in Morristown, New Jersey.

Frankie A, as his boyhood buddies often called him due to his superb intellect, had no interest in singing, but he did have aspirations to become a cop like his Dad. His three older sisters had sheltered, pampered, and supported him for most of his adolescent life.

Frank attended a Catholic elementary, middle school, and senior high school and excelled through every grade. He graduated from high school as co-valedictorian of his senior class and earned an academic scholarship from St. Elizabeth College, a Catholic co-educational institution.

Immediately following high school graduation, Frank enrolled at the Morristown campus of St. Elizabeth and ultimately graduated from there with honors. He received a Bachelor of Arts Degree in Criminal Justice.

Frank's initial plan was to pursue a career with the New Jersey State Police, but after talking to several of their recruiters, he alternatively joined the United States Navy. Frank wanted to become a commissioned officer, and at age twenty-one, he applied for and attended Officer Candidate School in Newport, Rhode Island. After graduation from OCS, he signed up for a four-year active duty commitment and was assigned to the Criminal Investigative Division in the Department of the Navy, headquartered in Norfolk, Virginia.

He was excited at the prospect of serving his country, in a demanding and important capacity, working undercover for the CID. However, during his first year, he became somewhat disillusioned about working undercover.

Frank remembered his first case as a newly commissioned Ensign. He was assigned to catch a postal clerk who was suspected of illegally disposing of official United States mail addressed to sailors, whom the clerk did not like.

The suspect was stationed aboard a World War II Gearing-class destroyer equipped with anti-submarine weapons, which was on patrol in the Mediterranean Sea. The CID had received several complaints from some of the enlisted crew members that they were only sporadically receiving their personal mail. Giordano had been assigned to work as a seaman on the deck force, responsible for all cleaning functions near the post office.

Frank investigated and eventually caught, a third-class postal clerk throwing mail, along with the office trash, overboard at night. The postal clerk was immediately arrested and escorted off the ship to a United States naval base in Rota, Spain, for a court martial and military processing. A week later, the ship was temporarily docked in Naples, Italy, for repairs. Frank was transferred and reassigned to another case from there.

Later that year, he was tasked to investigate a serious charge of theft, and the illegal sale of government property, by a commissioned officer. After the CID had been notified concerning discrepancies on internal inventory reports for cigarettes and other items being warehoused in the storeroom of a Naval Commissary, the CID decided to investigate. The supply officer in charge of the facility was named as a possible suspect. After several weeks of investigating, Frank arrested the Lieutenant, who was responsible for the facility. During an exhausting interrogation, the Lieutenant finally admitted his guilt, disclosing that he had regularly taken various items, including cartons of cigarettes, and sold them to an outside civilian contact. The officer received a court martial, was dishonorably discharged, and sentenced to five years in a federal penitentiary.

Three years later, after Giordano had been promoted to the rank of Lieutenant Junior Grade, he became involved with more serious types of crimes, including one espionage case. Despite the fact that his assignments had become more intriguing and significant, he decided to leave the military once his active duty had been completed.

Following his discharge, Giordano took a two-year position as a security director for a large manufacturing firm. The pay was more than adequate, but it was far less challenging than being in the United States Navy. Frank yearned for an exciting, dangerous, and fulfilling assignment, but he did not think the New Jersey State Police would fulfill his aspirations either.

He had pondered many times about becoming an FBI agent, so when the opportunity arose, he applied with the Bureau's counter-terrorism division. With his military experience, and degree in criminal justice, Giordano was quickly approved for admission into the FBI Academy. After graduation, he became an agent and was assigned to the Washington, D.C., headquarters office.

While working in Washington, he met Marie Mangione, an attractive younger woman who worked for the United States Department of Commerce. Within a year, they married and purchased a small but comfortable home in a nice middle class neighborhood in Arlington, Virginia. The couple resided there for over twenty years before Frank was reassigned to Grand Rapids.

At 5:00 p.m. that evening, Frank departed his office for home. He wondered about his future in the Bureau. *If only I could do something significant, like uncovering a terrorist cell or stopping a terrorist plot, I may be able to redeem myself,* he thought. *Unfortunately, there is not a snowballs chance in hell of that ever happening.* As he climbed into his vehicle and started the engine, Giordano found himself chuckling at the thought of those scenarios ever occurring in Grand Rapids, or, for that matter, anywhere else in Southwest Michigan.

Chapter 3

The following morning, as Giordano sat at his desk, he again reflected on the past events in New York City. He wondered where al-Qaeda would strike next. Surely they would pick another means to attack the West. Using airplanes would always be a viable option if it could be worked out. He was concerned; another successful attack on a large United States city would create more panic, devastation, and death.

Frank's greatest fear was that terrorists might someday try to detonate a nuclear weapon in a highly populated area, which would annihilate countless Americans and cripple the United States figuratively, financially, and emotionally.

Giordano hoped that would never happen, but he also understood that Jihadists were capable of the task. Jihadists were believed to be deranged by most in the civilized world and by the moderate Muslims as well. However, they were very dedicated to their cause, even though most of the "moderate" Muslims could not accept the "lessor" Jihad (a military conflict or holy war) and the indiscriminate killing of innocents as justifiable within The Qur'an (the primary holy text of the Islamic faith).

Giordano, and others in the agency, assumed that most intellectual people felt the vast majority of Muslims were honest, hand-working, and peaceful. Moderate Muslims had a very different understanding of the teachings about Jihad in the holy Qur'an, than did the radical Islamists'. However, in a literal sense, the call to Jihad, as written in the Qur'an, is applicable to all Muslims, including the moderates. Frank understood that in a religious context, "Jihad" had many meanings. It was often referred to as an external effort or internal struggle to become a better Muslim or believer in God. Over time, he became aware that some thought this concept was a modern construct to make Islam seem more palatable to the Westerners.

Giordano heard that at least one particular radical group, The Muslim Brotherhood, had promulgated a strategic plan for North America through a process called the "settlement alternative." It was referred to as the "Civilization-Jihadist Process." This process, according to the Brotherhood, was a kind of grand Jihad designed to eliminate and destroy Western civilization from within and sabotage its miserable house by their hands and the hands of their believers. Their goal was to eliminate Western civilization so that Islam is made victorious over all the other religions.

The Muslim Brotherhood is an Islamic organization founded in Ismailia, Egypt, by Hassan al-Banna in March 1928. It is an Islamist religious, political, and social movement. The group has spread to other Muslim countries; although, it has the largest following in Egypt. It has been the largest, well-organized, and most disciplined, political opposition force in the country. The Society of the Muslim Brothers, better known as the Muslim Brotherhood, is a transnational Sunni Islamist organization. The organization gained supporters throughout the Arab world and influenced other Islamist groups, such as, Hamas, with its "model of political activism combined with Islamic charity work." The Brotherhood is dedicated to the establishment of a nation based on Islamic principles. It has become a radical underground force in Egypt and other Sunni countries, promoting strict moral discipline and opposing Western influence, often by violence.

As claimed by the Brotherhood, without this level of understanding, Muslims are not up to the challenge and have not prepared themselves for Jihad yet. It is the Brotherhood's view that it is a Muslim's destiny to perform Jihad and work wherever he is or wherever he lands until the final hour comes. There is no escape from that destiny, except for those who chose to slack.

Ultimately, by establishing various Muslim societal organizations in North America, they are doing what is most important for Muslim's to do, claim The Brotherhood. Their task is to build and put forth a Foundation for the settlement alternative. The settlement process will be acted upon by coming generations who will finish the march but with clearly-defined guidance. These ideas were disturbing to Giordano, yet he knew it was going to be North America's long-term challenge to overcome the Brotherhood goals.

*   *   *

Frank had read some of the reports as to the possible whereabouts of Osama bin Laden but thought it would be very difficult to locate him, no matter where he was hiding. The United States intelligence agencies believed bin Laden was hiding in the mountains of Afghanistan. Nevertheless, due to the vast and rugged mountainous terrain of Afghanistan, Frank wondered where they were looking and if he would ever be found.

Frank was astounded at the ability of unrefined men, living in a third world country, being able to execute an incredibly destructive plan on the greatest country in the world, from thousands of miles away. Bin Laden had money, incredible support, and blessings from many in the Arab world making it all feasible.

Frank knew that America had been involved in the Middle East for decades largely because of the United States desire for oil from the Persian Gulf countries. The United States presence there, and the interference of the West in many of those countries governments, was a primary reason al-Qaeda, and the other splinter Jihadist groups, existed. Also, world dominance and the institution of Sharia Law were believed by the radical Islamists to be demanded in the Qur'an by Allah, (the one and only God in Islam). Plus, America supported, cooperated, protected, and armed the Zionist State of Israel and that was extremely troubling and unacceptable, particularly to the Palestinians'. Al-Qaeda also did not approve of the United States military presence in various countries within the region, particularly in the Suez Canal and the Arabian Sea.

Radical Islamic terrorist groups like al-Qaeda believed that the only way to rid themselves of the non-believing foreigners was to declare Jihad against them, which Osama bin Laden and Ayman al-Zawahiri did, along with three other Islamic Leaders, in 1996. A fatwa (a binding religious edict) was issued by bin Laden's group that neither bin Laden nor al-Zawahiri had the authority to authorize without the traditional Islamic scholarly or theological qualifications required. Nevertheless, they did it anyway. They considered the Westernization of their world by the United States to be decadent. In addition, they showed their utter hatred for Jews, Christians, Hindus, and all non-believers in Allah through their interpretation of the teachings of the Islamic faith.

September 11 was not the first-time radical Islamic terrorists had attacked the West or America. The "Great Satan," as America has become known as, has experienced prior attacks, both at home and abroad, for decades. The attacks on September 11 have been the most famous and devastating to date.

*   *   *

In a secluded and mountainous area, sixty miles north of Jalalabad between Kabul and the Pakistani border, a group of important al-Qaeda leaders hide in a large cavernous place, hunkered down for their own safety. Jaabir Muhammad, Anwar Hassan, and Faarooq Kazi were there, plus a small trusted security force. They were staying there temporarily while trying to blend in with the local Afghan's as their guests and under their protection.

Late at night, outside one of several caves at their encampment, sat a heavily clothed man in front of a smoldering bonfire. It was unseasonably cold and the moisture in the air permeated his skin. But, Anwar Hassan was used to the occasional harsh temperatures in the mountains. He was seated directly in front of the fire when another man appeared and said, "Good evening Anwar. God's peace is upon you."

Hassan responded, "And God's peace be upon you too my brother."

"May I share your fire?" asked Faarooq Kazi.

"Please, sit," instructed Hassan. "It is very cold this evening. Come close so we can talk about your special efforts in the United States. Jaabir and I have been deliberating options to follow the World Trade Center successes."

"Has he decided on pursing any of my proposals?" asked Kazi.

"Not yet, but the leadership is considering several of them. I wanted to confer with you first about your on-going operational plans for establishing sleeper cells in the United States. To date, how many have you established?" inquired Hassan.

"I have established, or I am in the process of finalizing, the relocation of several hundred brothers and sisters to six different communities within The Great Satan's borders."

"How were you able to establish them so quickly?" questioned Hassan.

"For more than ten years, handfuls of our sympathizers have been immigrating to the United States at different times and have become naturalized citizens there. They are no different than previous immigrants to America, like the Irish, Italians, Germans, and many others that came looking for employment opportunities to provide for their families. Once our sympathizers are established and identified, our recruiters contact them at their local Mosques and talk to them about our cause," said Kazi.

"Very interesting," commented Hassan. "How do you go about establishing cells?"

"Essentially, once the sympathizers have been converted and persuaded to support the cause of Jihad, we ask them to relocate in the approximate area where we want to set up a cell. They request family members and other like-minded brothers to follow them," explained Kazi.

"Where are they located?" asked Hassan.

"All of the proposed six cells are located approximately one hundred miles from the six largest cities in the United States, and I have plans to significantly increase that number within the coming year."

"Where is your oldest and most established cell located?" inquired Hassan.

"That would be the first one that I started working on. It's in a small town in Southwest Michigan called Langdon. Several of our brothers had been living in the

21

Dearborn, Michigan, area prior to their relocation to Langdon. I'm hopeful that cell may become operational within six months. Our main contact there is Najeeb Hammoud, a Sunni Muslim from Iraq."

"Tell me about Langdon," requested Hassan.

"Langdon is a small, rural farming community where approximately thirty Muslim families are currently residing. A few are dedicated sympathizers of ours, working and living in the community," said Kazi.

"What city is closest to Langdon?" asked Hassan.

"Chicago. Its population is about 2.7 million people. It is the third largest city in America and is located in their Heartland," stated Kazi.

"Yes, I'm familiar with Chicago. It would be perfect. The Americans are expecting another attack in the New York City or Washington, D.C., areas. I will discuss this with Jaabir and get back to you," Hassan said.

Upon leaving the campfire, Hassan said to Kazi, "Thank you Faarooq. Remember, we do as Allah wills."

"Yes, I understand completely," said Faarooq Kazi. "I'm grateful that Allah's blessings have been bestowed upon us all."

A few minutes later, the distinct sound of American Apache helicopters flying near their encampment caught Kazi's immediate attention. He wondered if they were there to drop off special operational soldiers to engage them in battle, destroy their temporary hiding place, and kill them. Fortunately for them, seconds later the choppers flew past their encampment and were out of sight. He breathed a sigh of relief. His desire was to remain alive long enough to kill as many Americans as possible.

It was 9:55 p.m., when Anwar Hassan approached an adjacent cave not far from where he had talked to Kazi. Outside the cavern, he could see a lanky, slender man bending down to pray inside the cave. The man was wearing a white turban and dressed in white and tan robes. Hassan waited awhile before entering the cave, so as not to disturb the man during his nightly prayer.

When Hassan entered, he was greeted by several guards positioned there to protect the thin, olive-skinned man with the voluminous brown beard and mustache. The man was now seated next to the campfire and barely moved when he heard his guards conversing. Immediately upon hearing Hassan's voice, the man turned and the face of one of the world's most wanted terrorist was visible.

In a soft voice, Jaabir Muhammad spoke politely and gestured to Hassan, "Come, sit next to me. We must talk," he said.

Hassan came and sat by the fire, as he was instructed to do by Muhammad. Almost immediately, Muhammad began to question him about what plans were underway for killing more Americans and their allies. Hassan knew that Muhammad, one of the senior al-Qaeda leaders was serious about this topic. Whenever there was any reference to the successes of the World Trade Center attacks, Muhammad, and the others would display wide smiles, but only briefly. They were more concerned about the future than the past. Anwar also knew Jaabir was a very patient man who insisted on adequate preparation, planning, and study before engaging the enemy.

After listening to Muhammad for several minutes, Hassan felt he was being given the opportunity to speak. Anwar, politely said to Jaabir, "I have been discussing some of our future operational proposals with Kazi, and he told me there is a cell in America being prepared to become operational in the next six months. It's very close to Chicago. In addition, he claimed he is working on five more cells that may be ready in nine months."

"Very promising," said Muhammad with a serious and studied look upon his face. "What are Kazi's thoughts?"

"He said he would like to use those cells as anonymous distribution centers for weapons, bomb making materials, ammunition, and communication devices. Those facilities could also be used to store operational money, and to store and produce U.S. identification papers for our Jihadist brothers and sisters."

"Would those cells provide warriors for our operational activities, or would they be there as anonymous facilitators?" questioned Jaabir.

"No, their mission would be to help enable others who will be trained to conduct the actual raids. Their autonomy would be of the utmost importance. Even our people conducting the raids would not know who they were or where the cells were located. Therefore, in the event our brothers may somehow become captured, the distribution centers would still be operational."

"Would we be able to ensure that the coordination and

communication components between the distribution centers, and our specially trained fighters, are workable without revealing or jeopardizing the distribution centers location?" questioned Muhammad.

"We are working on those details," said Hassan.

"How are we doing with locating and acquiring either biological materials or nuclear waste that could be incorporated in making dirty bombs?" Muhammad asked.

"We are working on those details too, but presently those things are not available to buy. We are trying to formulate a plan for Chicago, and the surrounding area, involving the cell in Langdon I had previously spoke of." said Hassan.

Once again, a quick smile appeared on Muhammad's face. "Keep me posted. I want to know when the plan has been completed and the cell is ready. I would like some time to study everything," said Muhammad.

"Yes, you will have our operational recommendations the minute Kazi and I feel they are ready for your assessment and approval," said Hassan.

Chapter 4

The community of Langdon is nestled in the rolling terrain of southwest Michigan and is largely made up of rural agricultural areas. It is approximately a half-hour drive from Lake Michigan and from the Indiana border. The area has various types of vineyards, blueberry farms, apple and peach orchards, truck farms, and corn, soy bean, and wheat fields. Langdon is typical of a normal farming community with the exception of the thirty or so Muslim families who co-exist with the predominately white farmers scattered throughout the area. Also, within the past five years, a small group of traditional Amish families have settled there to work in the factories and acquire farm land. It is an interesting mix for a town of roughly 1,500 people who reside in and around Langdon.

There are three factories in the area that provide jobs for Langdon's residents. One factory processes fruit juice, another manufactures boat trailers, and the last houses a steel fastener distribution center. There is a drug store, grocery, lumber yard, hardware store, and other retail establishments there as well. Langdon has one four-way traffic signal at the intersection of town. Also, there is a post office, Town Marshall's office, volunteer fire department, a half dozen protestant churches, and an elementary school. The junior and senior high schools are a combination of students from several smaller communities surrounding Langdon and are centrally located within the township.

Najeeb Hammoud and his family reside inside the city limits of Langdon. Najeeb is tall and extremely thin compared to the other Muslim residents. He has a thick brown beard, dark skin, bright shiny eyes, and a large prominent nose. He is normally friendly and smiles frequently. Najeeb always dresses in the traditional Iraqi Arab dishdasha (a long, white, loose fitting, shirt like garment) and an aba (long cloak, tan or neutral in color, for cool weather). Along with their clothing they also wear a kaffiyeh, which is a white or checked square scarf folded and worn over a small white cap on their head. The kaffiyeh is kept in place with a circular rope or cord called an agal. Men also wear undershirts and drawers, loose trousers, and a cotton or wool coat. Najeeb is a shrewd and skilled businessman, gifted in the art of gab and persuasion. It is no wonder that he has been so successful, in the past, at running retail establishments.

Daily, just before dawn, Najeeb arrives at the local musallah (a temporary mosque for Islamic prayer) and prepares himself to lead the pre-dawn prayers. Since he is the first to arrive at the musallah every morning, it is his responsibility to lead the prayer due to the absence of a local Imam (an Islamic worship leader who provides community support and spiritual advice). The make shift mosque, where the local Muslims come to pray, is located in a vacant building owned by Najeeb, and is adjacent to The General Store.

Najeeb, his wife Amira, and their infant child moved to Langdon in the summer of 2000, with the help and encouragement of an old acquaintance, Abdul Muqtadir. Abdul is an al-Qaeda sympathizer and organizer who temporarily helped Najeeb with financing, prior to the sale of his Dearborn store. Abdul's assistance allowed Najeeb to purchase The General Store, and the adjacent building next to the store, shortly after his arrival in Langdon. The seller was a long-time Langdon resident, who intended to retire to the gulf side of Southern Florida to play golf and fish.

Najeeb soon learned that the help he received from Abdul Muqtadir came with a price. He had agreed to help Abdul establish a sleeper cell in Langdon, which at the time did not seem to be too burdensome or dangerous. Previously, Najeeb had owned a small retail shop in Dearborn, Michigan, and it finally sold in the fall of 2000, several months after their relocation. Before purchasing The General Store, he had considered buying the local gas station too, but decided against it due to lack of funds.

Under Najeeb's direction, The General Store now stocks a selection of traditional Muslim and American clothing, small appliances, hardware items, fishing and hunting equipment and other miscellaneous items used every day in most households. In addition, there is a section devoted to boxed and canned goods, breads, locally grown fruits and vegetables, eggs, and dairy products. At first, Najeeb offered a small selection of Halal products (an Arabic word used to describe what foods are acceptable and permissible for consumption according to Islamic law), that were restocked twice weekly by vendors from Dearborn. As the Muslim population began to slowly increase in Langdon, Najeeb gradually increased the amount of Halal products available to meet the demand.

Hammoud and his family are one of the few Muslim families in town able to own an individual home. Most other newly arrived Muslims live in an apartment complex near the outskirts of town. All the Muslims are gainfully employed at one of the three medium-sized manufacturing plants in Langdon.

The Muslim children attend the various local schools. Some of the middle-school aged girls are unmistakable due to the traditional Hijabs they wear (veils worn to cover their faces), which is recommended under Islamic law. At puberty, both boys and girls are expected to dress more modestly. The Muslims' and their children are also easily identifiable because of their skin color and distinctive accents. The girls are to wear long dresses, however, and the boys can wear pants, shirts, and leather shoes, consistent with the other American boys.

For the most part, the Muslim men are very visible coming and going from their make-shift mosque, the factories, and the stores, either on foot or in their vehicles. They dress like the typical factory workers wearing shirts, along with blue jeans or workman slacks, and various types of shoes. Only a few men occasionally wear the traditional Muslim garb that Najeeb normally wears.

The Muslim women are not so readily seen, and the flippantly humorous rumor in town is that they are only allowed outdoors on Fridays. They wear the typical Muslim clothing, same as the pubescence girls, and are also required to wear the Hijabs. Occasionally, they are seen shopping at one of the major chain stores in the larger nearby city of Michigan City, Indiana, thirty-five miles southwest from Langdon.

Many of the Muslim residents are former friends or relatives of Najeeb's family. Most came to Langdon for the promise of a peaceful and safe environment, while at the same time, the likelihood of gainful employment that is not always available in the bigger United States cities. All of them are naturalized American citizens, and they are thankful for the neighborly reception they have received from most of the local residents and merchants. They are also reassured that their right to religious freedom is protected by the United States Constitution.

Most of the Sunni Muslims living in Langdon still have relatives in the Middle East. Most are fearful for their relative's well-being and lives. Sunni Muslims (one of the main sub-groups within Islam that follow the tradition of the Prophet Mohammed) originated from the question of who was to take over the leadership of the Muslim nation after Mohammed's demise.

More than eighty-five percent of the world's 1.6 billion Muslims are Sunnis. The main difference between the Sunni and the other main sub-group, known as the Shia Muslims, is political, not spiritual. In 632 A.D., a division emerged within the Muslim community shortly after the death of the Prophet Mohammed. He died without appointing a successor to lead the Muslim community. Consequently, disputes arose over who should shepherd the new and growing faith of Islam. The Shias believed they should have been the successors because of their heritage and not the Sunnis. Whereas the Sunnis felt a pious individual who would follow the Prophet's customs was acceptable.

Accordingly, Sunnis emphasize God's power in the world, sometimes including the public and political realms, while Shias value martyrdom and sacrifice. Sunnis also have a less elaborate religious hierarchy than Shias have, and they interpret Islamic law differently. According to Sunnis, humans are given an exalted status, which is given only to prophets in their holy book, The Qur'an. Clerics are venerated to Sainthood by the Shia themselves, whereas Sunni Muslims do not believe in applying the role of Saint to Clerics.

Najeeb Hammoud and the other Sunni Muslims are happy to be enjoying a better life than they had previously experienced in their former countries. At the same time, it would not be possible for them to break away from their traditional views and rules that bind them to their Muslim heritage and culture. After all, they are first and foremost Muslims, and they continue to believe in the Islamic teachings that they have grown up with. Of greatest importance in their lives is their constant belief in God and the opportunities given to seek His guidance and forgiveness.

All of Langdon's Sunni Muslims are considered

moderate, but several including Najeeb, are secretly sympathetic to the reasons the radical Islamists, in the al-Qaeda movement, are involved in Jihad.

Once the Muslims had lived and worked peacefully amongst the Langdon townsfolk for more than a year, most of the community members began to accept Najeeb and the others. Their fears about radical Jihadists living with them were finally being put to rest. It seemed apparent the religious diversity within the community between the Evangelical Whites, Anabaptists, Muslims, and the migrant Catholic Mexican workers, who journeyed to Michigan during harvest, was not a problem.

Hammoud liked living in Langdon, and his business was doing well. He was finally in a financial position to begin thinking about opening another type of business in the vacant, smaller building next to The General Store. Nonetheless, the Muslim community needed a local mosque, and his building was going to serve their community until another location could be found and was affordable.

He had thought about sub-dividing the building and renting the other side out, but he came to the realization that doing so would present a problem. Several of the Muslim men had offered to pay him a small stipend to cover the mosques operating expenses. Eventually, Najeeb took them up on their offer and split the expenses evenly amongst the other Muslim families.

Occasionally, there would be a few visiting Muslims from Dearborn in attendance at their mosque for prayer. On a very rare occasion an Imam from another mosque in a larger community might come to lead them in prayer too.

Najeeb had talked several times to his former Imam from Dearborn, whom he knew had ties to those very sympathetic and supportive of the al-Qaeda organization. Najeeb currently felt though that he had no reason to immediately support or promote the al-Qaeda cause.

He felt far removed from the problems and military conflicts affecting his former hometown, back in Iraq. Despite the fact that Saddam Hussein was an awful dictator, Najeeb's relatives, who were all Sunni's too, had not suffered under his reign, because they were sympathetic to many of his policies. Besides, Saddam had given Sunni Muslims all the important government positions, power, and influence over the Shia. In spite of the fact that the Shia made up the majority of the population of Iraq and the Sunni Muslims represented only twenty percent of the population. Najeeb and the others knew it would be very problematic for the Sunnis, to say the least, if the Shia were ever to regain power in Iraq and seek reprisals against the Sunnis.

There was talk concerning the possibility of the United States someday invading Iraq, deposing Hussein, and putting in a government more aligned with the United States government, but thus far it had not happened. As long as Saddam was in charge of Iraq, the Shias would continue to remain powerless.

Chapter 5

Abdul Muqtadir checked into a small, shabby looking motel near downtown Grand Rapids. He awoke the next morning at 6:00 a.m., said his prayers, showered, and got dressed. Muqtadir looked like the typical foreign-born, successful businessman. He always wore expensive looking business suits, drove fancy Mercedes Benz vehicles, and seemed moderately friendly to the average person he would encounter on the street.

Despite the fact that Muqtadir looked the part of a successful foreigner, there was a darker side to him that most rational people would never want to meet. He was not physically attractive, had sunken dark eyes, and at times, had the frightful stare of a viper ready to strike. He smoked and had very dark greasy skin that lead to a poor complexion. Nevertheless, Muqtadir was solid, and built like a Sherman tank, even though he was short and appeared to be slightly overweight. He was one of those types of people that you could encounter in a dark alley and immediately feel uncomfortable. He rarely smiled and was genuinely a disturbing looking character.

At 10:00 a.m. he took a cab to a real estate broker's office in downtown Grand Rapids. Earlier in the week, he had responded to a local newspaper advertisement concerning the rental of an apartment in the Grand Rapids area. Unfortunately, that apartment did not suit his needs. So, today, he and real estate agent Sandra Underlinde were going to look at several other apartments to rent. He was looking for an apartment in a quiet neighborhood where a safe house could be set up, to accommodate a newly appointed agent. The agent was several weeks away from finishing the al-Qaeda training program at a facility in Dearborn, Michigan. Abdul needed to find a safe place for the trainee to live and work temporarily, upon completion of the training. After several hours of looking, Abdul settled on a small studio apartment in the Grandville area. He paid a security deposit and signed a one-year lease, which he also paid for in cash.

Abdul had been living in the Dearborn area for more than ten years. He was self-employed and claimed to be an independent sales representative for several manufacturing companies. In truth, he had been involved with al-Qaeda, and other mid-eastern Jihadi groups, for a long time. His job was to receive and give orders, organize radical sympathizers, handle and recruit new al-Qaeda operatives, and to make recommendations to terrorist planners. For instance, in 2001, he had been involved in the successful attacks in New York City on 9/11. But, Abdul had managed to stay under the radar after the attacks, simply because the saboteurs had no idea he existed. They had received their orders from someone else.

When Zacarias Moussaoui was apprehended and

interviewed by the FBI, he had no idea of the existence of Abdul Muqtadir. Eventually, his testimony became helpful in piecing together all the names of the players involved in the attacks on the Twin Towers. Moussaoui had no idea Muqtadir existed because al-Qaeda's mode of operation was to allow only a handful of their most trusted members to be exposed to the full details of an operation. Minor players, like Moussaoui, were only told what their part was in an operation. Keeping the minor players in the dark is what helped make their undertakings so successful and difficult to penetrate.

Chapter 6

Early one morning, Giordano was in his office, reviewing a case file for an illegal drug network being investigated in Grand Rapids, when he received a call from his boss, Tom Murrell. "Frank, this is Murrell. Come up to my office right away please; I'd like to speak to you," he said, sounding unusually official.

"Sure, I'll be right there," Giordano responded. *I wonder what he wants.* A few minutes later, Frank got out of the elevator and approached Murrell's office door.

Murrell was a large, middle-aged, black-haired, Caucasian man who had worked for the Bureau for years and was well-respected. Upon hearing footsteps, he looked up and saw Giordano's well-developed figure approaching in the hallway. When Giordano arrived at Murrell's office door, he knocked and was quickly invited in.

"Good morning sir. What can I do for you?" said Giordano, upon entering the room.

"We need to talk," said Murrell.

"Okay," Giordano responded, quickly shaking

Murrell's extended hand before sitting in one of the upholstered chairs in front of the desk.

"Thanks for coming. I'll get right to the point Frank," he said. Murrell, who had a reputation for not messing around with small talk, began immediately talking business. "I believe I've made a mistake not involving you in more of our cases. I've been reviewing your personnel file again, and I'm a little confused. You had a stellar record as an agent, prior to the situation with the Moussaoui case in Minnesota. Do you want to tell me what happened with you?" requested Murrell.

"Would you like to hear the official version or my side of the story?" asked Giordano.

"Well, I've read the official version. It seems clear, from the FBI's documentation that you failed to fulfill your responsibilities as a special agent. Why didn't you properly file the Moussaoui report as you were expected to do?"

"That is the official version," stated Giordano. "The real story is, I did what I was supposed to do, and so did the agent I replaced. The problem, in the eyes of the FBI, was the supposed mishandling of the Moussaoui report."

"Would you please clarify that for me Frank?" requested Murrell.

"You see, the original investigating agent, Steven Pallone, had received a promotion within another division of the Justice Department. After Moussaoui had been captured, arrested, and charged, Pallone's final responsibilities were to write a detailed report about the case and forward it up the chain of command. Prior to his departure from the Bureau, I personally read the report and was assured he would see to it that the file was given to our superior, in a timely and proper manner. However, our supervisor denied ever receiving the report."

"I see," responded Murrell, obviously interested in hearing more of the explanation. "Did you check with Pallone as to whether or not it got filed?"

"Yes, Pallone verified to me that he had filed it properly. As Pallone's replacement, the responsibility to follow up on the case was left to me. I had nothing to do with preparing the original report," stated Giordano, in his own defense.

"Why would your supervisor deny receiving it?" inquired Murrell, soundly slightly skeptical.

"I don't know, but the chatter amongst my subordinates was that he was on the hot seat with his superiors and was being aggressively questioned about the entire Moussaoui incident. I can only assume he decided to cover his butt by blaming someone else," speculated Giordano.

"Can you prove that?" questioned Murrell.

"Unfortunately, I cannot. However, the FBI's assessment as to my lack of action was technically correct. I did not forward the original files in a timely and proper manner, but I know my predecessor did. I'd like to think the report accidentally got lost in transition, by our supervisor, and that his denial was an honest misunderstanding. But, if his superiors were threatening his job, I guess I could understand what might have motivated him to indicate that it had not been done properly. Once I was made aware of the problem, I immediately forwarded a duplicate copy of the report to my supervisor. However, I admit, it was after the fact," stated Giordano.

"Go on," said Murrell.

"I never knew the full scope of the problem with my supervisor until a month or so later, just before I was informed of my transfer," said Giordano. "In fact, I would have never known what was really going on if it hadn't been for a friend who spoke to me about what she thought had transpired."

"Okay," said Murrell, seeming to be more sympathetic at this point.

"When I learned that I had been unfairly blamed for the error, I approached my supervisor about the incident. Officially, he denied any involvement in the proceedings and claimed my accusation originated from above his pay grade. He suggested I could file a grievance, which I did. During the grievance meeting, I was told it was normal procedure to rotate agents after a problem with another agent had transpired."

"Alright," stated Murrell. "Did you ask to talk to the Director in charge of your division?"

"Yes, I talked to him, but he only repeated what my supervisor had previously stated. When I met with the Bureau's personnel department, they informed me about the reassignment. At first, they made it sound as though I was being presented with a lateral move. I mistakenly assumed I was being transferred here to head up this office.

After twenty-plus exemplary years with the Bureau, I never expected to be faced with this predicament. It was quite a shock, an embarrassment, and well … personally very disappointing," admitted Giordano.

"I'm sure you felt abandoned and unfairly treated," said Murrell.

"Initially, I thought about quitting the Bureau, but after the transfer, I changed my mind." Giordano said.

"I'm glad you changed your mind," said Murrell. "Whether you know it or not Frank, our case load has been increasing rapidly ever since September 11th, and I'm sure it is going to get much worse. The Bureau is currently asking all of its offices to take a second look at selected cases, specifically involving Muslims. Before you say it, yes, I know this is profiling and discrimination, but as long as we don't talk publicly about our methods, the higher-ups are fine with it," said Murrell. "For right now, they just want results."

"That's encouraging because those terrorists who commandeered the planes, and flew them into the twin towers, were not Protestants or Catholics. Finally, we will be allowed to use common sense, intuition, and experience to selectively profile Muslims when investigating potential terrorist crimes. Since September 11th, I've often wondered how long it would take for the Bureau to institute this change," stated Giordano.

"Well Frank, that's why I wanted to talk to you. Since you have experience in counter-terrorism, I thought you might be ready to head up an investigative unit for this office. I have a record of all U.S. Muslim citizens, Muslim business owners, and Muslims living in the U.S. on VISA's, where their mosques are located, and the companies who employ them in our jurisdiction area. In addition, I have criminal incident reports involving Muslims living in our area over the past five years. Can you get started immediately?" asked Murrell.

"Yes, I can start right away, and thanks for the chance to prove myself," said Giordano gratefully. "I really appreciate this opportunity and intend to be completely thorough and professional in my investigations."

"Sounds great Frank, and good luck," said Murrell. Another thing, I received a report the other day regarding a potential terrorist plot promulgated by the Central Intelligence Agency. It is a highly classified advisory paper generated by their counter-insurgency staff, which they are reluctantly sharing with the entire federal intelligence community. According to the report, one of their operatives, close to a major al-Qaeda planner, claims the organization wants to set up anonymous cells close to major cities in the United States. The purpose of those cells is to help facilitate terrorist attacks. The report claims they want to use legitimate businesses as fronts for those activities," stated Murrell.

"I'm not surprised. Their plots always seem to be very innovative, carefully crafted, and generally unexpected. I often wonder if they have spies in our midst. They always seem to know our weaknesses."

"It does seem rather peculiar sometimes, doesn't it? I

am doubtful though that we have many spies in the Bureau that we need to worry about," said Murrell, with a degree of seriousness in his voice. "I've got the listings that I told you about here on my desk. I'll turn them over to you along with the CIA report," Murrell said, as he handed the stack of papers to Giordano.

"Thanks again," said Giordano, extending his hand to Murrell.

"Now, let's get to work and see if we have any radical terrorists to be concerned about here in Southwest Michigan," he said, as he aggressively shook Giordano's hand.

"I'll start immediately," said Frank again, sounding excited that he was finally being given an opportunity to head up an investigation. Frank was surprised and knew he would be fully committed to the assignment. He imagined Marie would be pleased to see him enthusiastic about his job again, regardless of the excessive amount of investigative time the assignment will require. Murrell was perplexed when he looked up to see Giordano still standing in front of him as if something else remained on his mind.

"Do you have any questions Frank?"

"No, not right now, but I was wondering if you would be able to give me someone to help with the investigations? I assume this assignment will require a lot of man hours to complete."

"You're probably right," said Murrell. "Could you train Neal Johnson, the newbie, to help with the investigations?"

"I don't see why not," said Giordano. "He should work out just fine. Thanks for the manpower and your vote of confidence in me."

Chapter 7

Frank arrived early at the office the following morning. He had spent most of the prior evening thinking about how he might organize the investigation. After gulping down another cup of coffee, he began listing all the cities and towns that his office was responsible for on several large wall charts. He planned to record all the pertinent information that he had received from Murrell, under each applicable city or town, to see if there were any obvious connections. In addition, he decided he would visit each community, starting first with those towns that had any criminal incidents involving Muslims.

It took several days to transcribe all the information from the lists he had been given. It was apparent there would be plenty of data to look at after Frank began analyzing the information.

When he was not reviewing the data, Frank began thinking about the types of methods he might employ in his investigation. Surveillance techniques would be utilized only after first making contact with a suspect, who seemed to be potentially threatening. Frank had learned to be very aware of his surroundings and the people he would come in contact with.

Giordano knew he could normally ascertain whether or not a subject was lying to him during their initial interrogation, but he assumed Neal Johnson could not. Over the next several days, he began to refresh Johnson's memory about various surveillance techniques taught at the FBI Academy. Also, he explained to Johnson, the basic principles of how to identify deception during an interrogation.

"Criminals, terrorists, persons of interest, or ordinary citizens generally all feel uncomfortable when approached by the authorities," he told Johnson. Giordano instructed Johnson in the many scientific ways agents can detect deception, mostly through observation and interrogation. He told Johnson, "When being deceitful, most people become extremely nervous, particularly during questioning by agents. I will also go over other obvious signs."

Giordano asserted, "Most interrogators will tell you that it is harder to keep a story straight when the suspects have inserted lies into their statements rather than just trying to remember the truth. Asking similar questions to a suspect in different ways is a good method to catch them lying, when they try to give their statements.

Giordano also claimed, "Most agents pay close attention to how a person's eye movements appear during questioning. They are mindful of inappropriate facial expressions, how a person's body language changes, and how the tone of their voice may vary during an interrogation. Also, if a person is sweating or flushed, those signs may also indicate a person is lying. One more sign to look for is, if a person is constantly looking down during an interview that generally indicates the person is not telling the truth," said Giordano. He assured Johnson that through experience most field agents can be quickly and adequately trained to identify the many telltale signs of deception. Nevertheless, Giordano knew career criminals might be more difficult to detect than the average person. It was also common knowledge that many terrorists had previously been trained in the art of deception.

As an experienced former counter-terrorism specialist, Giordano told Johnson that basically their job was to connect the dots, in order to find the terrorists. He indicated that in essence that was Counter-Terrorism. If they gathered enough personal information and history about a suspect, and incorporated interrogation, surveillance, and wiretapping, to examine them, Giordano knew they would find out whether or not their suspect was a terrorist. The challenge was to make that first connection, whether by blind luck, hard work, or a little bit of both.

Giordano intended to use some of the more basic techniques taught by the Bureau that had been used in the field for years. One particular program he especially liked was created and used by the CIA during the Vietnam War. The program acquired intelligence on subjects either after they were caught or suspected of participating in covert operations. Special career South Vietnamese soldiers, trained by the CIA, were used as "Action Arms" to capture, interrogate, and turn enemy combatants against the insurgency.

Periodically, Giordano involved Johnson in the planning phases of an investigation, and he routinely kept Murrell well informed as to his progress. Giordano planned to utilize Johnson and himself as "Action Arms" in their interrogations and investigatory procedures, very much like the South Vietnamese soldiers had been trained to do, by the CIA.

To date, they had not been able to uncover any credible leads or situations pointing to a terrorist activity or plot. Candidly, Giordano hoped to be able to uncover something sinister, which would help rebuild his standing with Tom Murrell, as a good and reputable FBI agent.

Before accepting Neal Johnson as his partner, Giordano had unofficially asked Murrell to look at his personnel file. Murrell was not surprised by the request considering he too had done the same thing in the past.

As Murrell was filling out the Bureau's compliance report concerning the establishment of an investigatory unit for the Grand Rapids office, he felt pleased. Giordano was perfect for the job, and the addition of Johnson could not have worked out better. It would be helpful that Johnson spoke Arabic too. Giordano had also been pleasantly surprised when he saw the potential qualifications Johnson would be bringing to their investigatory unit.

It was as if it had been planned by someone at the FBI headquarters. The thought amused Murrell, knowing it was not possible.

Johnson was born into a mixed Arab/African American

military family in the mid-eastern country of Yemen in 1975. His parents were James Johnson, a deceased career Marine, and his wife, Saarah Nazir-Johnson. James had been assigned to the United States Marine Corps detachment at the United States Embassy in Yemen to protect Matthew Tueller, the United States Ambassador, and to guard the facilities. Saarah was a Yemeni and was employed by the Embassy as a department interpreter and clerk. They met while working there and eventually fell in love and married. Neal was born less than a year after their marriage in Yemen. When Neal was ten years old, the family moved to Raleigh, North Carolina, and purchased a small home there. Prior to their move to Raleigh, James had been stationed at other military bases both in the United States and internationally. When Neal turned eighteen, he enrolled at Shaw University in Raleigh, which is the oldest historically black college in the South. Four years later, he graduated with honors.

Prior to his death, Neil's father, James, had been strongly encouraged to retire by the Marine Corps after serving more than twenty-five years. He was told he would be mandated to leave the military sooner rather than later due to a security clearance issue and his resultant inability for advancement.

A year later, after being forced to retire early, James' retirement benefits suffered due to his lack of advancement possibilities. Saarah and the entire Johnson family thought he was not being treated fairly. They were not at all happy about the way the government had handled his retirement. Several of his immediate family members encouraged him to file a discrimination law suit against the United States

Marine Corps.

From the beginning, Saarah had never accepted his predicament and had insisted James contact the ACLU and the NAACP for help. After several unsuccessful attempts to obtain damages, the government eventually offered a meager compromise to James, in order to avoid controversy. He wanted to accept the compromise, but Saarah wanted to continue fighting the government. The battle went on for more than three months before a renegotiated compromise was accepted. During that time period, the United States military became a constant disappointment for the entire Johnson family.

In spite of the problems, Neal's mother, Saarah finally became a naturalized American citizen. She continued to speak English and both classical and modern standard Arabic (the universal Arabic language) fluently. She taught her son Neal, as he was growing up, to speak Arabic fluently as well.

Giordano was puzzled when he found out that Johnson had been assigned right out of the FBI Academy to work in southwest Michigan. With Johnson's background, Giordano was curious about why he had been assigned to work in Grand Rapids, instead of in the highly populated Muslim community near Detroit, Michigan. The chances of uncovering a terrorist plot, locating a clandestine al-Qaeda group (also known as a sleeper cell), or stopping a terrorist attack seemed remote in Grand Rapids. But, after his experiences with the Bureau, he was beginning to wonder whether or not the decision makers were capable of doing a credible job anymore. If he were in charge,

Johnson would have been immediately assigned to work in the Detroit office.

In addition to Johnson's ability to speak Arabic, he also understood the typical Muslim lifestyle, with regard to Islam, because of his own life experiences and upbringing. Furthermore, he knew the do's and the do not's regarding what was permissible within the Muslim culture. All in all, Giordano seemed extremely positive about their ability to uncover any sign of terrorist activity in their on-going investigations.

Due to the sizable number of Muslims living, working, and operating businesses in the greater Grand Rapids area, Giordano decided to begin his investigation there first. It was tedious work, but Johnson's ability to communicate in Arabic helped to move things along rapidly. They learned there were only a couple dozen criminal complaints against Muslim men in Grand Rapids over the past five years. The fact that this number was so low surprised Giordano. Johnson, on the other hand, was not surprised at all and reminded Giordano that Muslim men typically stick to themselves, are family oriented, and have an abiding faith. Since Islam does not allow for the consumption of alcohol, normally men do not frequent bars or associate much with non-Muslims. Generally speaking, most of the problems involving Muslims were associated with assaults on them by Michiganders, who were either intoxicated and/or had a prior record of harassing immigrant families.

To his surprise, Giordano learned from Johnson that there was a certain tolerance by moderate Muslims for other religious persons who believed in one God, as

Muslims do. Giordano also learned, many Muslims consider atheists or non-believers as void of any spirituality and religion. However, Johnson said most moderate Muslims were willing to accept the non-believers in Islam, without feeling the necessity of killing them if they chose not to convert. Conversely, the radical Islamists thought all non-believers in Allah needed to be either converted or put to death. That essentially was one of the many underlying reasons for the 9/11 attacks, along with their utter dislike for Western culture, their military involvement, and their commercial interference in the Arab world.

Giordano found Johnson easy to talk to, well informed about traditional Muslim values and practices, and knowledgeable about procedural expectations within the Bureau. Johnson was a fast study concerning surveillance, interrogation techniques, deception awareness, and information gathering. After working several weeks in the Grand Rapids area, Giordano began to acknowledge their efforts to date had not been very successful. Most of the Muslim men they had encountered appeared to be hard working family men who were devoutly religious and model citizens.

That is not to say that all of Giordano's and Johnson's efforts were unproductive. They had discovered there was a group of younger Muslim men in Grand Rapids involved in illegal drug activity for a well-organized Hispanic gang. Giordano noted his findings and filed a report with the local drug eradication unit. They proceeded with their investigations believing the young Muslims' involvement with drugs had no connection to terrorism.

Frank understood that looking for a terrorist cell could be like looking for a needle in a haystack. On the other hand, he also knew that it only took one good lead, and they could be on their way to uncovering terrorist activity. They had investigated Muslim businessmen who employed other Muslims but had uncovered nothing significant. Mostly, unskilled Muslims were employed in factories or as cab drivers, gas station clerks, or general laborers.

Johnson and Giordano interviewed many of the Muslims that had been included in Murrell's list. For the most part, they concluded Muslims were happy living in America. They were thankful to be given the opportunity to take care of their families, educate their children, and to be protected by the rights given in the United States Constitution. In general, they found American Muslims were concerned about the absence of Sharia law (a set of religious principles which form part of the Islamic tradition) in the United States. Nevertheless, most Muslims still lived their everyday lives, as though it did. Johnson explained to Giordano that it was every Muslim's obligation to live a Sharia compliant life but that did not include any perceived obligation to try to impose Sharia on others.

* * *

A month and a half later, following a discussion between Hassan and Muhammad concerning the establishment of terrorist cells in the United States,

Muhammad was informed that the CIA had issued a report regarding this exact matter. It was speculated that these cells were to be used to help facilitate terrorist attacks in America. Muhammad was not only surprised by the CIA report, but also by the unsettling idea there may be an informant inside al-Qaeda leaking information. Hassan cautioned Muhammad and the group not to immediately treat the report as a sign that a traitor was operating within their organization. Instead, he suggested they limit access to their operational planning group, and do nothing that might legitimize the CIA's claim as to the existence of terrorist cells inside American. He suggested that the report may have been written as a logical consequence following the attacks on the Twin Towers and the Pentagon. Hassan believed the American government was likely fishing for information to see if they could uncover any plots by floating out bogus reports. Muhammad agreed but decided to tighten up access to his inner-circle and their operations just in case there was a traitor in their midst. Hassan suggested that even if there was an informant, the knowledge of his existence could be used to provide their enemies with misinformation. He went on to reason, if there was a traitor, which he doubted, why had their location not been compromised, and why had they not already been attacked by the Americans.

Chapter 8

Grandville, Michigan, nestled along the shores of the Grand River, about fifteen minutes southwest of downtown Grand Rapids, is an easy place for a clandestine operator to blend in. Grandville boasts a plethora of parks, miles of hiking and biking trails, and is one of Grand Rapid's largest shopping and dining districts. It is the perfect setting where outsiders can come and enjoy the community's small-town feel, preserved in such rituals as holiday parades, firework displays, and other community celebrations.

In a small, inconspicuous studio apartment, amidst one of the quieter neighborhoods in Grandville, sits an al-Qaeda agent utilizing a computer to enter information. The agent had been instructed by her al-Qaeda handler to periodically e-mail an activity report, including potential target opportunities and their perceived weaknesses, to an anonymous email address. It was also the agent's assignment to try to provide an overall assessment of the local police agencies, security forces, FBI, and statewide Homeland Security teams surrounding two of Michigan's nuclear power facilities. Important intelligence, periodically acquired by the agent, would also be communicated in this manner.

The agent had been working secretly for the past several months and is currently utilizing the Grandville apartment as needed. All expenses and costs, including the apartment, are being provided by Abdul Muqtadir, (Najeeb Hammoud's old friend from Dearborn). Muqtadir is one of only a few handlers for the al-Qaeda organization residing and working in the United States. Presently, the newly activated agent was working in the Grand Rapids area and had been radicalized and motivated to help the al-Qaeda leadership to fulfill their mission against the United States of America. The agent's motives were simple: obtain revenge against the United States government and be well paid for doing it.

Muqtadir tasked his newest agent in Michigan to obtain as much information as possible about the two nuclear power plants in the Southwest Michigan area. The first plant, located near South Haven, is called Palisades Nuclear Generating Station and is the oldest nuclear plant on the Eastern shore of Lake Michigan.

The second plant, The Donald C. Cook Nuclear Power Plant, is a newer plant located just north of the city of Bridgman, on a 650-acre site. The plant is owned by American Electric Power and operated by Indiana Michigan Power, an AEP subsidiary. It has two nuclear reactors and is the company's only nuclear power plant. It produces enough power to meet the needs of a city with a population of 1.25 million.

The Palisades Nuclear Generating Station is a nuclear power plant on a 432-acre site in Van Buren County, five miles south of South Haven. It is operated by the Nuclear Management Company and is owned by CMS Energy Company. Their Westinghouse Electric Company turbine generator can produce 725,000 kilowatts of electricity.

There is a third nuclear power plant in Michigan located near the east side of the state on the Shore of Lake Erie. The Enrico Fermi Nuclear Generating Station is near Monroe, in Frenchtown Charter Township, on a 1,000 acre site. It is owned by DTE Energy and operated by DTE Energy Electric Company. The three nuclear plants combined supply one-quarter of the power needed for Michigan residents.

Originally, the newly trained agent, Ashley Khan, had been contacted by an al-Qaeda sympathizer who had heard that the potential recruit might be persuaded to help al-Qaeda. After the recruit was introduced to Abdul Muqtadir, there was an initial personal investigation conducted. It took several months of checking family background, verifying her authenticity, and conducting intense questioning before the potential recruit was approved to join the clandestine al-Qaeda team. Khan had told Muqtadir about her past activities with another Islamic group, years earlier in Yemen, including when she had killed a Marine guard while working at the United States Embassy.

Once the killing was verified, her credibility went up immensely with Muqtadir. After the initial approval process, the newcomer received several months of basic training courses in al-Qaeda's operations. This basic training included clandestine training, communication skills, lethal weaponry training, and some general undercover surveillance skills. This training was required before she was released to do active covert assignments, under Muqtadir's supervision.

Khan's first assignment was to gather information for a plan being considered by al-Qaeda that involved one of the Michigan nuclear power plants. Her assignment was to help bring the plan to fruition. The strategy they shared with her was to overtake a facility by surprise attack, hold hostages, demand millions for agreeing not to destroy it, and to obtain free passage for the perpetrators, once the ransom money was received.

However, the real proposed plot, which was not presently being communicated to Khan, called for a complete takeover of either plant. Following the takeover, they planned to explode the nuclear reactor or reactors, causing many residents in Indiana, Illinois, and Michigan to be exposed to highly damaging radioactive material. The real purpose of this mission was to kill or injure several thousand Americans. Al-Qaeda knew once a nuclear facility was exploded, there would be a fireball, a shockwave, and intense radiation. A mushroom cloud would form from the vaporized debris and disperse radioactive particles that fall to earth. The radioactive particles would contaminate air, soil, water, and the food supply. When carried by wind currents, the fallout would cause far-reaching environmental damage.

Muqtadir intentionally also failed to mention to Khan

that the Jihadi fighters, who would be training for the mission, were going to be committing suicide, just like their brothers had done at the World Trade Center.

The later plan that was not communicated to Khan was a hypothetical operational plan that Faarooq Kazi, one of the al-Qaeda's planning chiefs, was working on. Nevertheless, she understood she was working on a fact finding mission to help Kazi fully develop, communicate, and gain approval for yet another particularly destructive al-Qaeda operational plan. Muqtadir hoped, if enacted, the plan would be potentially far more disastrous than 9/11 or any other plan had been, thus far.

Khan understood her assignment was only hypothetical and wondered if she was being fully informed about the whole plot. She chose not to speculate whether it would actually occur or if her lack of knowledge really mattered. So, for the time being, she was going to follow Muqtadir's instructions, regardless of the projects feasibility or acceptance.

*   *   *

It was just before 5:00 p.m. when Giordano and Johnson pulled into the FBI office complex in preparation to end their shift and go home. It had been another busy day spent interviewing, and although the work was getting done, they still had not uncovered any wrongdoing by those they had investigated.

There was an unusual calmness about Giordano that

Johnson had observed more than once before. He found it hard to understand. At one point, Johnson had asked Giordano about his calmness and seemingly endless patience. Giordano responded, "It's just something you will get used to. You see, the vast majority of our investigations will be boring until you develop that first lead that cracks the case wide open." Johnson commented back that in his opinion they were not going to find much of anything on this case. He was surprised by Giordano's follow-up response of, "Let's just wait and see." Johnson wondered if there was any pertinent information Giordano knew that he wasn't sharing.

After the normal end of day wrap-up conversation, they agreed to meet the following morning for breakfast in order to begin fine tuning the next phase of their on-going investigation in Grand Rapids. Many of the personal interviews had been completed, but there were several that Giordano wanted to follow-up on, based on his intuition. They decided to conduct surveillance on some of the interviewees to verify some of the statements that several of them had made, during their interviews.

As Johnson was getting ready to exit their shared office space, Giordano's telephone rang. Giordano sat back down at his desk to answer the call. Johnson was going to wait for Giordano's call to end before departing until he heard Giordano say to the caller, "Please, excuse me for a moment." He saw Giordano place his hand over the receiver and said to him, "This is a personal call Neal. See you in the morning. Okay?"

Johnson acknowledged saying, "See you at The Greasy

Spoon."

Frank responded, "Sure thing, see you at 7 a.m."

Johnson wondered to himself if there was something wrong. *Who was the caller, and was there any significance to the timing of the call?* He thought he noticed a look of surprise on Giordano's face, when he first answered the phone.

Giordano waited for several seconds to ensure his partner had departed the office before resuming the phone conversation. Giordano listened as the caller talked. Occasionally he would respond with a "yes sir" or a "no sir." The phone conversation went on for the next few minutes until the caller said "goodbye," and Giordano hung up the phone.

After the call ended, Giordano sat motionlessly in his chair pondering the unexpected conversation, the revelations, and the ramifications to him. He could not believe what had just been revealed and the potential dire consequences surrounding the situation. The subject matter was very secretive, and the caller had naturally advised him not to discuss the conversation with anyone.

A few minutes later, Giordano turned off his office lights, locked the door, and headed home. He thought about telling his wife about the conversation, but he had been trained by the Bureau to do no such thing, for her protection, as well as his own. On the commute home, he continued to think about the unexpected call, and thought to himself, *what was their rationale in accusing me of doing something I did not do?*

Chapter 9

Early the following morning, Giordano lay in bed reflecting on the call he had received the prior afternoon. He wondered how he could keep track of Johnson without attracting too much attention. The caller indicated the Bureau would provide needed assistance. Frank assumed that would mean there would be back-up surveillance teams monitoring Johnson's activities, outside the office. Giordano decided to verify his assumptions the next time he reported in to the Washington Bureau Chief.

Johnson was a highly trained FBI agent. Giordano realized, over the past week, that he had been helping Johnson to improve his awareness skills. His former counter-terrorism division chief had concerns about Johnson being a spy. Giordano wondered why the FBI did not inform him of their suspicions, or their plan to catch him, before now. It seemed to Giordano that the Bureau had approached this matter incorrectly from the very beginning. *But, who am I to question my former boss' judgment or actions?* he thought.

Frank arose early, showered, and readied himself for

his breakfast meeting with Johnson. He seemed unprepared but decided the big-shots had hand-picked him for a reason; they apparently believed in his ability. *What an inconsistency, considering at one point, I had almost been banished from the Bureau,* thought Giordano.

On his drive to their favorite Greek restaurant, which Giordano had nicknamed the Greasy Spoon, he decided to behave as if he were an actor playing a part. It was a technique taught at the FBI Academy. This technique allowed agents to learn how to behave differently than normally expected, free of emotional involvement, in order to conceal their real agendas. In other words, he would play the part of the loyal, cooperative friend and co-worker to Johnson, while at the same time gathering evidence to use against him if warranted. Giordano was hopeful that his superior skill set would keep Johnson from being able to see right through him.

Giordano was certain that Johnson was unaware he was fluent in Arabic. He had never bothered to inform or demonstrate to Johnson this capability. He had been allowing Johnson to do all of their Arabic interviews, in order to teach him how they should be done. Giordano handled the English interviews. He was certain that by allowing Johnson to conduct most of the interviews, it would help him to gain valuable experience in dealing with potential suspects. Giordano had always made it a policy not to divulge too much information about himself to a new partner, at least not until he had built a trusting relationship with them. In this case, that decision showed to be a wise one.

Understanding Arabic was a task Giordano was encouraged to acquire while working in the counter-terrorism division. Having the ability to understand a conversation, spoken in a foreign language, and without the suspect knowing about it, had proven useful in the past. All counter-terrorism agents were encouraged to learn at least one foreign language. Not only was Giordano fluent in Arabic, but he could also understand Russian as well. Even though Johnson had never been attached to the counter-terrorism division, Giordano wondered if Johnson would consider the possibility that his new supervisor might be fluent in a foreign language, specifically Arabic.

It was 7:15 a.m. when Giordano entered the Greasy Spoon. He noted Johnson had already arrived and was drinking a cup of coffee in the corner booth. When Johnson noticed his presence, he got up and waved at Giordano to attract his attention. Giordano greeted him with the same negative comment he had always made to him every morning by saying, "Thank God for coffee. I hate mornings." Johnson was a morning person, but it was quite evident that Giordano was not.

Occasionally Johnson would respond, "How did you ever get through the military or the FBI Academy if you hated mornings so much?"

"I guess back then it wasn't such an issue," he admitted. "Probably old age has finally set in," Giordano said, gruffly. "Come talk to me when you're my age, and tell me if you haven't changed your mind about mornings."

"You're probably right," he said. "What's on the agenda for next week Boss?" asked Johnson.

We'll talk about the schedule after breakfast," Giordano said, grumpily.

"Alright then," Johnson said politely. *I can't believe how edgy he can be sometimes, and at other times, be so low-keyed. I hope I'm not as crabby when I get to be his age,* he thought.

Johnson was in his mid-twenties, well-built and tall, with skin color uncharacteristically light brown. This was unusual for a person with a mixture of black and Arabian genes. He sometimes wondered about why he was not darker, but concluded that his heredity was to blame. *Unbeknownst to my family, there must have been some white chromosomes somewhere lurking in my DNA,* he thought. Johnson was handsome with a perfect completion. "I must have gotten that from my mother," he would say if someone commented to him about his skin color and good looks.

From a very young age, he had always wanted to be employed by the United States government in some capacity, like his father had been. *What an opportunity to be an active FBI field agent responsible for and exposed to lots of important information,* he thought. He knew if his father were still alive today, he would be very proud of most of his accomplishments, but maybe not all of his decisions. Unfortunately, his father was not alive, and the family continued to accuse and blame the military for his premature death. Johnson had been adversely affected by his father's passing. His feelings about the United States government had somewhat changed after seeing how the Marine Corps had treated his Dad.

Chapter 10

Driving south along Red Arrow Highway, the newly trained, female al-Qaeda agent, code named Ashley Khan, was going to visit Grand Mere State Park for a two-day information gathering excursion. The name Ashley Khan was fictitious, but nonetheless, the agent had been given supporting documentation to prove it was not. Fake names and documents were all part of the al-Qaeda plan to confuse the authorities in case of capture. Abdul Muqtadir, her handler, had arranged for all the details of Khan's indoctrination, training, activation, and supervision.

The park was located very close to Stevensville, Michigan. The plan was to explore the southernmost desolate area of the park, with the hope of being able to see the Cook Nuclear Power Station. Originally, Khan had planned to tour Cook's visitor's center but was disappointed to learn that since the September 11 attacks, those tours were now only available to school groups.

Regardless, the libraries in the communities of Bridgman, St. Joseph, and Stevensville had provided Khan with substantial background information about the nuclear facility. Prior to her visit to Grand Mere, she had been on a fishing excursion that passed by the nuclear facility's western side. Khan had used a camera with a high powered lens to photograph the facility from the main deck of the fishing boat. Captain Kevin O'Leary, the boat's owner and operator, paid little attention to his customer's photographic subject matter and seemed more interested in getting the tourists out to the best fishing spots.

The visit to Lake Michigan brought back fond memories for Khan of days passed in a different time and place. It was a beautiful sunny day, and the calm, cool waters of Lake Michigan glistened in the sunshine. It was not uncommon for tourists to carry cameras to record their experiences and the beautiful scenery present in the early part of Michigan's autumn season. The variety of trees, with their colorful leaves that intermingled in the forests, were remarkable and attracted as much attention as did the other sites at all the Michigan State Parks. In addition to the stunning views, park visitors also enjoyed the sandy beaches, the cooling Lake Michigan waters, and the night-time family campfires always prevalent in early September.

Prior to visiting Grand Mere, Khan utilized the safe house computer to gain more information about the Donald C. Cook Nuclear Power Plant facility. One such online article stated that inside the Cook Nuclear Power Plant visitor's center was a 26-foot animated model demonstrating how the plant operated. Unfortunately, this was no longer accessible by the general public. She did find some interesting data still available about the nuclear facility. For example, the population statistics showed that 58,000 people lived within a ten-mile radius of the facility and 1,191,827 people resided within a 50-mile radius. She thought those statistics would be interesting for the al-Qaeda planners to know about, so she recorded them in her notebook.

The internet showed no statistics on the number of people employed by the Cook nuclear facility, but Khan was certain it averaged more than 100 per shift. Aside from the clerical and managerial staffs, the facility employed general cleaning service contractors and lawn care specialists too. The facility also employed full-time utility cleaners inside the reactor areas, communication personnel, nuclear chemists, nuclear maintenance supervisors, electrical engineers, and reactor operators. Additionally, there was an adequately sized fire, and security staff.

The Cook facility was situated in hilly terrain, amongst the Lake Michigan sand dunes. Three sides of the facility were occupied by dense woods and pine forests. The west side of the facility bordered Lake Michigan. The nuclear plant was set back 75 feet from the shoreline, and there was a water retention cement wall running parallel to the main plant facility. The few windows the facility had were all situated above the ground floor level. The complex was well illuminated with observation stations that were all manned by armed guards. The main facility housed two nuclear reactors that were in operation 24-hours a day. There was a ten foot chain-linked fence surrounding the entire complex, with sensors. The employee parking lot was located alongside the two-lane roadway that leads into the facility from Red Arrow Highway. The parking lot and the roadway also were enclosed by the perimeter fencing.

The facility was directly accessible from the interstate, which allowed police and security personnel from nearby towns to get to the facility in less than ten minutes.

The state park encased 985 beautiful acres that geologically surrounded three ancient inland lakes. After entering the park, Khan was given a site map and a sheet with rules and regulations before she settled on a campsite as far south as possible. It took about five minutes to set up the tent at an isolated camp site that looked as if it had not been used in years. The park was forest covered and full of sandy terrain, which was very cumbersome to walk through. Grand Mere State Park had two miles of sandy beaches located on the eastern shore of Lake Michigan.

About an hour later, following an exhausting climb, Khan was able to see a portion of the Cook facility from high atop a sparsely pine covered sand dune. The binoculars, and a highly magnified camera lens, helped the agent to observe and obtain pictures of the physical plant and the surrounding campus. From that location, portions of the back side of the facility, including the parking lot, the roadway, and several adjacent buildings, were clearly visible.

There were two guards stationed in each of the four observation towers, along with a manned checkpoint at either end of the road that helped to safeguard the facility. All guards appeared to be armed with military type rifles and each also carried a pistol. That meant if a covert force were going to gain access to the facility from Red Arrow Highway, they would have to open the fence manually and overtake two separately guarded checkpoints in order to get into the area.

Khan noted that there was another fence of at least ten-feet surrounding where the nuclear reactors were housed, inside the already enclosed area. There was a sandy buffer of twenty feet in between the fence and the building, probably equipped with motion sensors too. This meant that no matter where you approached the nuclear facility from, there were going to be at least two fences to traverse in order to gain access to one of the two rear plant entry doors. It was apparent that this facility was well equipped with plenty of formidable fencing, substantial illumination, highly armed personnel, sensors, and natural barriers designed to impede entrance onto the grounds.

Even if a highly trained team of al-Qaeda saboteurs were able to get inside the grounds, they would still have to gain access to the nuclear reactors through an almost impenetrable three-foot concrete wall, which Khan had read about online. The task seemed all but impossible. The agent wondered if the Palisades Nuclear Facility, which was an older nuclear facility near South Haven, would be more easily accessible.

Terrorists in the Heartland

Chapter 11

It was a bright sunny morning as Hammoud eased his van into the small parking space between his two buildings. He walked around to the front of The General Store and stopped briefly to admire his property. *What a great acquisition*, he thought. He was thankful that Allah had given him so many blessings. Aside from the business, he and his family had an opportunity for a peaceful and plentiful life in Langdon.

Since Hammoud arrived first at the mosque, he unlocked the door and made preparations for the morning prayers. Like clockwork, the Muslim men in the community filed into the mosque shortly after his arrival. He was a little startled to see the daunting face of his old friend, Abdul Muqtadir, among them. Hammoud presumed he was in Langdon to talk to him about the arrangement. It had been several months since he had been in contact with him, and Hammoud was very nervous about his visit.

After the prayers had been concluded, and all the men left for their jobs, Hammoud greeted Muqtadir. "How are you feeling my brother?" asked Hammoud. "The last time we saw each other you were recovering from an upper respiratory infection. You seemed to be very sick," he stated. "Are you taking any medication?"

"My doctor says I have asthma, but I don't believe him.

I refuse to take the medicine he has prescribed. Listen, before we go back to your office and talk, I'd like to see where you plan to create more storage capacity," Muqtadir insisted. Hammoud led him to the upstairs attic space and explained his renovation plans. After touring the space above The General Store, they went down to Hammoud's office for a cool drink and to briefly talk about their families. After several minutes of pleasantries, Muqtadir stated the real reason for his visit was to talk about their arrangement. "Have you discussed our plans with any of your friends yet?" he asked.

"Not yet, but I will," said Hammoud. It is not the right time."

"What does that mean?" Muqtadir blurted out, with an immediate heighten burst of emotion, which was totally in character for him. "Do you recall our arrangement? It was based on the understanding that I would help you, and in turn, you would help me. I provided you with enough money to buy this business and your home, and now it is up to you to help me set up a sleeper cell."

"Yes, I know that is what I agreed to do," said Hammoud, quickly acknowledging his promise.

"What is the problem then?" questioned Muqtadir. "You know I have made promises to your al-Qaeda benefactors. This sleeper cell is to be operational in a few months. I believe they have begun to make plans that involve your cell specifically."

"Abdul, please be patient," said Hammoud, calmly trying to appease him. "I am still committed to the cause, but I have to admit, I am nervous about getting involved right now. Things are going very well for us here in Langdon. These people look up to me and rely on me for their welfare. This country has been very good to them so far. If you could give me more time, I am sure that we will be able to proceed as planned. I simply need more time to prepare the others for the important work ahead," declared Hammoud.

"I would like to give you more time, but I too am operating on a schedule. I can assure you, this cell will not be susceptible to much danger," stated Muqtadir frankly. "Your people will not be directly involved in any covert terrorist activity. The cell will only be used as a supply depot for our Jihadi fighters and will be anonymous even to them. The only people who will know of your location, purpose, and existence will be me, and a few key al-Qaeda leaders. I will provide the supplies; your job will be to warehouse them. When supplies are needed for an operation, I will arrange to have them picked up and delivered to the fighters. Your function is to hide the supplies, and keep them safe. I believe the additional space you identified will be adequate for us," Muqtadir told Hammoud.

"Yes, I am sure we can secure all the things you will need in the attic of The General Store. However, the attic will need modifications in order to make it work,

Hammoud responded. I think we will be able to conceal the supplies in those two small shrouded areas that I have shown you. Nevertheless, I am very concerned about taking this risk. I believe it is asking too much from us right now. There are several in our community that are sympathetic to al-Qaeda, but I will need more time to convince them to become involved," explained Hammoud.

Muqtadir arose, leaned down, and looked directly into Hammoud's eyes with the most sinister stare he could produce. Clearly, distinctly, and calmly he said, "Najeeb ... you and I have been friends for a long time. I have never let you down, and I do not expect that you will let me down. Many of our brothers and sisters have made far more sacrifices on behalf of al-Qaeda, Islam, and Allah than I am asking of you. Do not let me down," Muqtadir said again, in a very intimidating and insistent way. His tone and manner sent a chill through Hammoud that he would not forget for a long time. The longer Muqtadir talked the redder his face became. For the first time in his life, Hammoud was more than alarmed by Muqtadir's behavior.

Hammoud waited several seconds before he responded. Drawing upon all the courage he could muster, he said, "Abdul ... you know I will do whatever needs to be done in order to help you."

"I know you will old friend, but if you do not, there will be serious repercussions for you, and your family," Muqtadir said sternly.

"I understand. You do not have to worry." Hammoud assured him. Beads of sweat slowly began to drip down the side of his face as he was speaking. Najeeb Hammoud was visibly intimated, frightened, and scared. Muqtadir had a reputation for being a very sinister and conniving person, capable of anything, including murder.

Chapter 12

After reviewing the back of the Cook facility, it took Khan about an hour and a half to walk back to her campsite through an adjacent wooded area at Grand Mere State Park. Disturbingly, she noticed upon her return, that there was a park ranger's vehicle stopped alongside her rental car. A middle-aged park ranger was looking through the windows of her small sedan, trying to see the contents inside, when Khan spotted him. The al-Qaeda agent wondered what the park ranger was doing and why he was there. Deciding to wait a few minutes before returning to the campsite, the agent ducked behind several pine trees to observe. After what seemed like an eternity, the chubby park ranger returned to his vehicle looking as if he were preparing to leave. Instead, the ranger quickly emerged with a clip board. Khan watched through her binoculars, as the ranger began filling out a form.

After several minutes, Khan decided to return to the campsite to find out what was going on. Just prior to her arrival back at the campsite, she unbuttoned the top two buttons on her blouse to reveal a generous glimpse of her cleavage, which she hoped would be pleasing to him. The intentional action of exposing herself to him was wrong for a Muslim woman to do, but she did it for a purpose.

The ranger looked up upon hearing the sound of someone coming through the dense pine forest. He put the clip board down on top of the vehicle's trunk and awaited the person's arrival.

Khan slowly approached the ranger from the woods, and said, "Good afternoon officer," trying not to startle him. At the same time, she tried to act as innocent and friendly as possible. "Is there something I can help you with?" she inquired. *I will have to lie to protect myself,* thought Khan. *Unfortunately, I'm caught. She remembered seeing the warning signs posted on the roadway and knew she should not be there. I hope I can somehow sweet talk my way out of this predicament.*

"Good afternoon," said the park ranger. "Would you mind telling me what you are doing in this area of the park? Didn't you notice the signs restricting access over here?" asked the ranger, in a very serious tone.

Hesitating briefly, the agent responded, "Yes, I did see the signs officer, and I'm very sorry. You see, I selected this campsite because it looked to be more desolate than the other sites on this side of the park. In my line of work, I was hopeful it would be more productive to stay here. I'm a free-lance professional wildlife and nature photographer, and for the last several hours I have been shooting some incredible wildlife photographs. No doubt you have probably seen some of my photographs published in various magazines. My name is Ashley Khan. If you like, I can send you some of the better photos once I've developed the film?"

"No, that won't be necessary, Ms. Khan, but thanks anyway," said the ranger. "How long have you been in the park?" he asked.

"I've only been here for a few hours. Is there a problem officer? I hope you haven't been waiting too long for me to return."

"No, I just arrived and since this area is restricted that is why I stopped to investigate. You know there is a nuclear power plant adjacent to us, on this side of the park. That's why access is limited," he said, candidly.

"I did not know that," responded the agent, innocently.

"Could I see your driver's license please?" asked the officer. "Also, I'll need to confiscate all your film and there will be a fine for not complying with our rules."

"I'm really very sorry," she said again, trying to appease the ranger. "I didn't realize there was a problem in being on this side of the park, and I certainly didn't think what I was doing was wrong. Could you give me a break just this once? I don't make very much money as a photographer. I'll gather my things and be out of here in a couple of minutes," she said, trying to be polite and persuasive. "No one will be the wiser."

"I'm really sorry Ms. Khan. I'd like to help you out, but if I don't file this report, I could get myself into big trouble," said the park ranger, firmly. "If I could have your driver's license and the film cartridges, you will be allowed to go on your way in about thirty minutes," stated the ranger.

"Thirty minutes?" she exclaimed. "What else do I have to do?"

"Technically, you are being arrested and you will have to accompany me to our on-site office, where you will be required to pay the fine," said the ranger.

"I see," she said. "I believe my license is in my backpack along with the film." The agent removed the backpack and placed it on the ground in front of the officer. "It might take me a moment to find my license," she said sweetly, as she bent over. She assumed her partially covered breasts were visible to him. At least she hoped so. It was an attempt to entice the ranger to do what she wanted him to do for her; forget about the infraction. *Maybe the view of my breasts will be enough to allow him to give me a break just this one time,* she thought.

"Take your time," said the ranger. "I'm here uh … all day," he said, as he looked down at her partially exposed breasts. He felt slightly embarrassed and somewhat perverted, as a devout Baptist, to be staring at her chest, so he quickly looked away.

Khan found the license and slowly grasped it in one hand while skillfully palming her pocket knife in the other. Here's my license officer," she said, as she got up and handed it to him. The ranger took it, quickly turned back toward the rental, grabbed the clip board, and began filling out the report. "Are you sure you can't forget about this?" asked the al-Qaeda operative once again.

"No, I'm really sorry Ms. Khan," said the soft-spoken

park ranger. "I'd really like to help you out, but I can't. The fine is not very much," he said.

"Alright, I understand," she said calmly, as she slowly began to move toward the ranger. Khan managed to quietly and stealthily flip open the blade on her pocket knife, without attracting the ranger's attention. Seconds later, she grabbed him from behind and swiped the sharp blade across the unsuspecting park ranger's throat. The knife easily severed his right juggler vein as it sliced into his neck. Within seconds, a steady stream of blood was visibly spurting out of him, in unison with his heart beat. Immediately, upon feeling the sensation of the blade slitting his throat, and seeing the blood gushing out of his body, the ranger gasped, turned, and attempted to look into the agent's eyes. Hastily, he tried to stop the hemorrhaging, but to no avail. Realizing the effort was futile; the ranger fought with the agent and tried to subdue her, while reaching for his service weapon. Skillfully, she grabbed the man's hand and held it in place, as he attempted unsuccessfully to remove his weapon from the holster. It only took a short time before the officer became unconscious, dropped to the ground, and lay dead in a large pool of his own blood.

Without panicking the al-Qaeda agent retrieved her driver's license and the film canisters, got into the ranger's vehicle, and slowly drove it a short distance through the sand near the pine woods, to the edge of a deep ravine. She revved the engine, left the vehicle in drive, and then quickly jumped out and helped to propel it down into the gorge. She waited until after the vehicle traveled to the bottom of the forty-foot ravine, before turning to leave.

Once the vehicle had crash landed in the ravine, it flipped over on its side and slowly began to emit smoke. When the agent took one final look at the truck, she noticed the wheels were still turning and the engine continued to run.

Afterwards, she hurriedly returned to the body and began dragging the corpse towards a smaller sand dune, away from the ravine. She returned to her rental car, and inside the trunk, she retrieved several large trash bags, which she used to contain the ranger's body. The agent enclosed the corpse into the bags and began looking for a cleft in the sand where she could hide the body. While dragging the body, she struggled several times, due to the ranger's excessive weight and her smaller statue. Once she located a small pit to place the body in, she dragged it in the hole and began covering it up with sand and available broken tree branches. Several minutes later, she returned to the campsite, cleaned herself up, and quickly changed clothes. Then, she nonchalantly loaded up her supplies, and the tent, into the trunk of the rental car, and departed Grand Mere State Park. As the car traveled down the interstate, the agent continued to check the rear view mirror to verify that there was no one following from behind.

Khan did not stop the car until she arrived back at the Grandville safe house. The agent had been trained to kill using either a knife, a gun, or employing her hand to hand combat skills. Nevertheless, the prospect of actually having to murder someone that day had not been contemplated for this task. Observing nuclear sites was not supposed to involve killing, nor did the task of gathering and communicating information to an anonymous email address hardly seem dangerous. The agent had been compromised and went into panic mode. She believed there was no other choice … the ranger had to die.

Khan was emotionally shaken by the necessity to kill. Then again, it was too late to undo what had been done. In the end, self-survival had motivated her to kill once again. Her involvement with al-Qaeda was a way for her to make the United States government suffer and to be reimbursed for the losses associated with her deceased husband's Marine Corps pension. This was the second time she had been forced to kill someone, while doing what normally would be considered a slightly dangerous, yet moderately easy task. In Yemen, she had been able to separate herself quite easily from the grasp of the Islamic extremists, but in the United States she knew it would be much more difficult.

She understood once the ranger's corpse and vehicle were found, the homicide would alert the authorities to the possibility that the park ranger had come upon someone involved in a criminal activity and had to be silenced for their protection. Khan hoped the authorities would not make a connection involving the nuclear plant, but understood that possibility existed. *Thank God I became proficient in self-defense a long time ago,* thought Khan. She took some time to shower and unwind from the traumatic events of the day, before sitting down to the computer to report the incident. *I need to be more careful going forward,* she thought.

* * *

The following morning, Muqtadir received the coded report from his agent concerning the death of the Grand Mere Park Officer. He was already aware of the officer's death from the reports, both on television and in the newspapers. Prior to Muqtadir reading the agent's report though, he had no idea the incident involved al-Qaeda or Khan. He was relieved when the authorities stated, there were no witnesses, and there appeared to be no motive concerning the incident. It was speculated that the park ranger might have unknowingly surprised someone involved in a drug transaction and was killed as a result. No definitive conclusion as to the motive had been reached, and the authorities were continuing to investigate the crime.

According to the local newspaper account, funeral arrangements were being postponed for a few days at the request of the investigators. The ranger was survived by a wife, three children, and five grandchildren. The article stated the park ranger had intended to retire within the year and was well-known in the community.

Muqtadir was thankful that his agent had not been captured and handled the situation remarkably well, considering the circumstances. After all, Khan had not been an undercover operative for very long, and it appeared that she had left no loose ends to worry about. Later in the day, Muqtadir sat down at his typewriter to prepare a coded message about the incident for his contact. Ultimately, he knew Anwar Hassan, Faarooq Kazi, and Jaabir Muhammad would be notified too. In addition, he wanted to relay the essentials of his disappointing conversation with Hammoud. Muqtadir decided to put his own misleading spin on their conversation, in order to look better, explaining about Hammoud's weak commitment to their cause and his reluctance to immediately get involved. However, Muqtadir did mention, to those in command, that Hammoud had pledged not to stand in their way, turn them into the authorities, or impede their advancement. Nevertheless, he was concerned.

Muqtadir suggested in his message to his al-Qaeda contact that he might provide Hammoud with a reason to get involved, by threatening his family either in Langdon or in Tikrit, his former hometown in Iraq. Muqtadir had already acted without gaining approval from al-Qaeda. He was hopeful that the al-Qaeda leadership would approve of his recommendations. Muqtadir did not want his superiors to know he had previously threatened Hammoud. He understood that in matters such as these, patience was recommended.

Muqtadir also reported that he had learned of an important development. The West was planning to attack Saddam Hussein and his regime, in the next several months. If this was true, he indicated he could arrange for Hammoud's relatives to be killed and make it appear as if it was the result of reprisals by the Shia Muslims. He was convinced Hammoud would blame the Americans, and their allies, for the death of his relatives. Muqtadir thought that Hammoud would then have a reason to help them and support their Jihadi cause. He would have to wait to hear from the al-Qaeda leadership before advancing any plan regarding Hammoud. Muqtadir was hopeful that he would hear a response sooner, rather than later. He had committed himself to having at least one of the sleeper cells completed. He did not want to disappoint his superiors back in Afghanistan, in case they had already decided on a plan and were ready to go with it.

Chapter 13

Stanley Whitman, the murdered Grand Mere park ranger, was buried a week later in a small, rural Stevensville Baptist church cemetery. He received the typical, well-attended law enforcement funeral service. There were many statewide law officers that represented different enforcement agencies in attendance, along with family members, friends, and local dignitaries.

Immediately after the murder was discovered, the story was widely covered by the news media. But, over the next several weeks those stories moved from the front pages to smaller follow-up stories on the inside pages of most area newspapers. Unless the case was quickly solved, or a new development was uncovered, the story would probably not reappear in the newspapers for quite a while. Ultimately, the headlines would shift to more pertinent news events.

The Berrien County Sheriff's Department was in charge of the on-going investigation. However, because of Grand Mere's proximity to the nuclear power facility the initial homicide report was sent to the State of Michigan's Police, Park, and Justice Departments, the FBI, and to the

United States Homeland Security Department. The FBI had been tasked to do a follow-up investigation of the homicide on behalf of the Bureau and the Homeland Security departments of the Federal government. The initial investigation rendered no definitive conclusion, and the Sheriff's department had their doubts that the ranger's death was connected to the nuclear facility. Giordano and Johnson were assigned to the case by Murrell, their supervisory agent, who wanted them to review the case evidence and report their findings.

Because Giordano was the senior agent, he was in charge of the investigation and responsible for the dissemination of a follow-up report to the Bureau and Homeland Security. When he and Johnson first arrived at the Berrien County Sheriff's Department, they received the usual cooperative greeting. But, Giordano knew the FBI's presence was not always looked upon favorably by the local authorities. Nevertheless, they were given the case file, access to the evidence, and escorted by a Deputy Sheriff to the crime scene at Grand Mere. Due to his past experiences, Giordano knew the crime scene had probably been trampled upon by other investigators. Plus, natural occurrences, such as, strong gusts of wind or rain could have altered the scene too.

Upon Giordano's arrival at the campsite, he noted there were still tire tracks leading off the asphalt road into the sand that had stopped at the edge of a deep ravine. The authorities had found the ranger's vehicle at the bottom of the ravine. At the crime scene, there were remnants of the blood trail found in the sand where the deceased officer had been dragged. The body had previously been removed, but there were police photos depicting the condition and location of the corpse. Also, there were pictures of the vehicle found in the ravine. The black plastic garbage bags used by the murderer to cover the body were in the evidence room of the Sheriff's Department, and the ranger's vehicle was in the department's garage being inspected. No finger prints were recovered from the garbage bags, the vehicle, or found on the body. No DNA samples, other than that of the deceased, were found at the crime scene. This led Giordano to believe the assailant must have been wearing gloves when the crime was committed. The other park rangers had not seen anyone looking suspicious, entering or exiting the park, that afternoon. Park visitors and campers were quickly contacted and questioned once the body was discovered, but no one reported seeing anything unusual. Perplexingly, no one could recall seeing Ranger Whitman prior to the time period when the crime was said to have occurred. The ranger had not reported anything unusual that afternoon and was presumably busy making his normal stops around the park. The ranger's vehicle had been thoroughly inspected and apparently had run out of gasoline because of the crash, sometime after it landed at the bottom of the ravine. Nothing out of the ordinary was found in or around the vehicle, except for an empty clipboard inside the Jeep that usually held a small number of park citation forms. Although, there were no citation forms found in the vehicle, the Sheriff's Department did delineate in their report that there should have been. Normally, the rangers carried them to write up violations, such as a camper who might have been found intoxicated in the park or violating a park rule or regulation. Giordano theorized that due to the absence of citation forms in the vehicle, the ranger might have been giving someone a ticket for a violation rather than coming up on someone committing a crime. Giordano thought that was probably the case and noted the irregularity in his report.

After reviewing the evidence, Giordano decided to continue pursuing the case, not only because he believed the ranger had not felt threatened at the time of the incident, but because he felt uncomfortable with the local investigator's conclusions. Even though, the absence of citation forms was documented in the original investigative report, their absence was determined to be of little significance. If his theory was correct, Giordano presumed that the ranger's assailant had possibly taken a completed citation form from the clip board, prior to his or her departure.

In order to try to recover any of Whitman's citation forms, a quick check of the park's dumpsters, local service station trash containers, and convenience store dumpsters was conducted by the authorities. Unfortunately, nothing was found. Security cameras, operated by businesses close to the park, yielded no suspicious looking footage either. There had also been no record during that time of anyone receiving a speeding violation within ten miles in either direction of the park entrance.

In several police photos, Giordano observed that the officer's service weapon was still in its holster, but its security strap had been unclasped. The autopsy had indicated some significant bruising on two spots of the officer's right forearm. It was determined that could have occurred as a result of a natural incident due to the officer taking Coumadin (a blood thinner) at the time of his death.

Admittance to Grand Mere State Park required either an annual park sticker appearing on the vehicle's windshield or a cash payment of ten dollars at admittance. Several admission passes were sold that day and were reflected in the park's cash record book. To Giordano's despair, there was no requirement for recording the names of those who purchased the passes. There were also no faces to identify, license plates to check, specific vehicle to search for, or security footage to review, because the park department did not have security cameras.

The coroner had concluded that death resulted quickly after the right carotid artery had been severed. The murder weapon, which was presumed to be a knife, had not been recovered. It was determined the weapon had been fairly sharp and the length of the blade was between three to four inches long. The weapon could have easily been a Swiss Army pocket knife used by many campers. Judging from the angle of the lacerations into the neck tissue, the coroner indicated the wounds were probably made by someone smaller than the ranger, who was five feet ten inches tall.

Not surprisingly, there were only a few visible clues at the crime scene. Giordano took note of several tire tracks leading in and out of the campsite, where the crime had apparently occurred. The police were trying to determine the make and model of any vehicle equipped with those type of tires. To date, they were still waiting on special investigators from the Michigan State Police laboratory to help make that determination. Also, there were several stake marks visible in the dirt and sand, presumably from the erection of a small tent at the campsite. No debris was found in the campsite's trash barrel. After further investigation, Giordano noted that the camper apparently had ignored two prominently placed "No Access" warning signs leading to the remote campsite.

Although there was no proof, Giordano believed the ranger may have died as a result of discovering that a spy or a foreign operative had breached the park's "no access" area that just happened to be adjacent to the Cook nuclear facility. He speculated the purpose might have been to get a good look at the layout of the facility, possibly with the intention to someday destroy it and create a nuclear disaster. Giordano included in his notes that it was entirely possible for someone to have climbed to the top of an extremely elevated, nearby sand dune to observe the Cook nuclear facility.

Giordano understood murders rarely occur in Michigan state parks. Most visitors were there to enjoy the beach, the scenery, and the camp ground with their families. The incident concerned him, particularly because it might involve the nuclear power plant. He understood that the local authorities were not accustomed to or expecting to find any involvement of a foreign entity at a state park crime scene. Unfortunately, working for the Bureau over the years had proven to Giordano that spies do these sorts of things more frequently than the public would ever believe possible.

*   *   *

Several weeks later, in the mountains of Afghanistan, a long-awaited courier arrived with several coded messages from important al-Qaeda affiliates. Those messages were hidden amongst supplies being transported by several trusted Afghan's using mules. There were messages about Muhammad and Hassan family member's, their welfare, and their current locations. Another was a report requested by Muhammad as to al-Qaeda's personnel recruitment efforts in Afghanistan and elsewhere in the Middle East. Lastly, there was a report from a United States clandestine al-Qaeda official detailing the progress made in regards to compiling information about the two Michigan nuclear facilities. The coded message was addressed to Faarooq Kazi.

In the operative's report, Kazi learned that a park ranger had been killed, by one of their newly activated agents, during a fact-finding operation. The report claimed that, as a result, there was an on-going investigation being conducted by the United States Federal government into the matter. Fortunately, the al-Qaeda official felt the agent had done a very good job dealing with the incident and had left few clues to help the investigators. He advised Kazi that he intended to wait a few weeks before trying to have the other nuclear facility inspected.

The official also communicated to both Kazi and Hassan the issue he was having setting up their first sleeper cell in a timely manner. He indicated that their contact in Langdon, Najeeb Hammoud, was getting cold feet in regards to helping them set the sleeper cell up, as he had originally promised. Hammoud was asking for more time to involve several of the other Muslim residents there and indicated the problem was the result of the residents becoming too satisfied with their lifestyles in American. According to the official, Hammoud had claimed he felt no immediate reason to move as quickly as they wanted. Despite Hammoud not moving quickly enough, Muqtadir told the al-Qaeda leadership he thought Hammoud could be persuaded to fully cooperate and would not jeopardize their operation.

Also, Muqtadir indicated that he had heard from an al-Qaeda operative, who had infiltrated the United States military, that there would be a full scale attack on Iraq sometime in early 2003, in order to depose Saddam Hussein and his regime. The informant, a United States Army guard at the Pentagon had innocently overheard a brief conversation between several flag officers outside a secure briefing room. The informant told his barracks roommate, who was an undercover al-Qaeda operative, about the attack. Both Kazi and Hassan were not surprised; they had been hearing the same rumors concerning the attack.

However, after reading Muqtadir's report, both Hassan and Kazi were furious with Hammoud. After all, they had provided him with operating money to purchase a home and a business in Langdon, and this was how he was repaying them. *Allah would not be too happy with Hammoud,* thought Hassan. *If he were not such an important player, I would immediately order his death.* Both Hassan and Kazi thought it wise not to mention the problems with Hammoud to Muhammad, who had little or no patience for anyone not willing to work with al-Qaeda.

In the official's message to the al-Qaeda leadership, he had suggested to Kazi that if the United States attacked Iraq, and deposed Hussein, there would be chaos in the streets. The Shia would more than likely seek reprisals against the Sunni Muslims. Muqtadir indicated that situation would present an opportunity and a reason for Hammoud to immediately comply with their requests, especially if his mother and two brothers came up missing and were presumed dead. He was certain Hammoud would blame the American invasion, and the Shia uprising, as the cause of their disappearances. Hassan was fairly certain that if something happened to Hammoud's relatives, he would be extremely angry, resentful, and vindictive towards the United States government. In their message back to Abdul Muqtadir, one of the United States clandestine al-Qaeda officials, both Kazi and Hassan advised him to let Hammoud live for now, at least until the cell was fully operational. Both men agreed his insubordination could be dealt with at a later time.

Terrorists in the Heartland

Chapter 14

Giordano and Johnson spent the next ten days carefully reviewing the evidence and investigating the death of Stanley Whitman, the murdered Grand Mere park ranger. The authorities were finding it difficult to solve the case with the existing information, but Giordano did not want to give up on the investigation. He did have his doubts however, without any further leads or evidence; he believed it may be fruitless to continue. He had developed a theory that the ranger had been murdered, by an anonymous operative, who had been caught gathering information on the Cook Nuclear Plant. Frank believed his theory was feasible, even though there was no hard evidence to prove it, only his professional experience and intuition. As the weeks past, the park ranger's case grew colder and colder. But still, the Michigan authorities continued to maintain an open file on Ranger Whitman's murder.

Giordano was frustrated. Hard as he tried, he could not find any connection to a terrorist scheme, drug deal, or criminal plot. The investigation uncovered no witnesses, suspects, finger prints, or unknown DNA samples. There were also no surveillance photos, vehicle descriptions, license plate numbers, or suspicious activity to pursue. The only useful evidence was the presence of several tire tracks that were found on the scene, presumably made by a 4-cylinder Ford Escape. The state police laboratory had determined that those tire tracks were from a 225/70R15 tire, a popular tire size used on Escapes and similar sized vehicles.

In his follow-up report to the Bureau and Homeland Security, Giordano reiterated his theory and disclosed that the suspect or suspects had probably been driving either a 2001 or 2002 Ford Escape. Giordano reported that he was putting the case temporarily on hold, until further information became available. He assured the Bureau and Homeland Security that he would quickly resume the investigation and notify them if anything significant developed. Until further leads were forthcoming, he told the Bureau that he would continue his on-going investigative efforts to uncover terrorist activities in Southwest Michigan.

All the while, Giordano had continued to monitor Johnson's activities and behavior, and to date, had not seen any sign that he was a traitor. In fact, the more he was around Johnson, the more he thought Johnson was a patriot. The Bureau also informed Giordano that based on their monitoring of Johnson, he had not demonstrated any suspicious behavior during his off-duty hours either. Giordano assumed there was a good reason for the Bureau's concern, but his former boss never fully explained the exact details for their suspicions concerning Johnson.

*   *   *

On October 2, 2002, President George W. Bush announced the issuance of a Joint Congressional Resolution to authorize the use of United States Armed Forces against Iraq in order to fight anti-American terrorism. Citing the Iraq Liberation Act of 1998, the resolution reiterated that it should be the policy of the United States to remove the Saddam Hussein regime and promote a democratic replacement. The resolution supported and encouraged diplomatic efforts by the United States to strictly enforce the resolution through the United Nations Security Council, and all their relevant resolutions regarding Iraq. The resolution also authorized the President to use all the United States Forces, as would be necessary and appropriate, to defend the national security of the United States against the threat posed by the Hussein regime. One month before the invasion of Iraq, Secretary of State Colin Powell addressed the United Nations Security Council concerning Resolution 1441. Resolution 1441 was most prominent prior to the buildup before the war. The resolution formed the main backdrop for authorizing an individual member state to use military force to compel Iraq to comply with the many prior Security Council resolutions.

After Bush's announcement, it was very clear to

Hammoud and Muqtadir, who along with the rest of the world viewed the Special Report on their televisions, that the United States was very serious about getting rid of the Hussein regime in Iraq. Hammoud was immediately concerned about the ramifications for his family, still living in Iraq, if Hussein was overthrown. Muqtadir was concerned as well but for very different reasons. He understood that once the Hussein regime was toppled, it would give al-Qaeda opportunity to quickly grow and expand their influence in the region. Muqtadir had already made arrangements with some al-Qaeda affiliates in Tikrit to get rid of Hammoud's mother and brothers, once outbreaks of sectarian violence started to occur in the Iraqi streets. Muqtadir's plan was designed to motivate Hammoud to immediately act on the arrangement he had entered into with al-Qaeda.

* * *

On March 19, 2003, President Bush again addressed the nation and announced the beginning of Operation Iraqi Freedom. In his pronouncement, Bush stated, "The people of the United States and our friends and allies will not live at the mercy of an outlaw regime that threatens the peace with weapons of mass murder." A United States Senate committee report later revealed that many of the administration's pre-war statements about Iraq's WMD's (weapons of mass destruction) were not supported by the underlying intelligence, after the invasion had occurred.

The 2003 invasion of Iraq lasted from March 20, 2003, to May 1, 2003. The incursion consisted of twenty-one days of major combat operations. During this incursion, a combined force of about 160,000 troops from the United States, United Kingdom, Australia, and Poland invaded Iraq and deposed the Ba'athist government of Saddam Hussein. The coalition forces also received support from Kurdish irregulars in Iraqi Kurdistan.

The stated coalition mission was to disarm Iraq of weapons of mass destruction, end Saddam Hussein's support for terrorism, and free the Iraqi people. The impact of the 9/11 attacks, and the role this played in changing United States strategic calculations, gave rise to the freedom agenda. Once the opening attack had occurred, it was anticipated that the elimination of the leadership would lead to the collapse of the Iraqi Forces and the government. It was assumed that much of the population would support the invaders once the government had been weakened.

Many observers felt that the Coalition Forces devoted a sufficient number of combatants to the invasion, but believed that too many were withdrawn after it ended. After the invasion, the failure to occupy cities put the Coalition at a major disadvantage in achieving security and order throughout the country, and local support failed to meet expectations. Once Baghdad fell, there was an outbreak of regional, sectarian violence throughout the country, as Iraqi tribes and cities began to fight each other over old grudges. United States led Coalition forces quickly found themselves embroiled in a potential civil war.

Just prior to the March 20 invasion, Hammoud had been in touch with his family members in Tikrit via telephone. Once combat operations began in Iraq, it was temporarily impossible to find out if they were safe or not. A month or more past before Hammoud was able to contact his first cousin in the neighboring town of Laqlaq, near Tikrit. His cousin told him that his relatives were missing and presumed dead. At first he did not believe it, thinking his immediate family members would emerge after the Coalition combat operations ended. He was aware of the estimated 7,300 Iraqi civilian fatalities that occurred during the invasion. As time passed, Hammoud began to accept the possibility that they had gotten caught up in the sectarian fighting and reprisals occurring in Iraq. Once they failed to reappear after another month, Hammoud believed that they were, in fact, dead.

Hammoud was emotionally heartbroken and extremely enraged with the thought of losing his family members, who had apparently died in Tikrit sometime during the invasion. He wondered if their bodies would ever be found and given a proper burial, or if they might have been buried in a mass grave, dug by the Coalition. Nevertheless, he was sickened, infuriated, and blamed the United States Coalition forces for their demise.

Up until now, Hammoud had delayed fulfilling his arrangement with Muqtadir and al-Qaeda to set up a sleeper cell, due to his fear of being caught working with al-Qaeda by the United States authorities. However, after his loved-ones mysteriously disappeared, Hammoud began making preparations to quickly establish and activate the sleeper cell in Langdon. At first, he wondered if Muqtadir somehow had been involved in their demise, but he quickly dismissed the thought as too outrageous to be possible. Within a few days, he met with three other potential al-Qaeda sympathizers within their small Muslim community, to discuss their possible affiliation and motivation to help al-Qaeda. As anticipated, Hammoud was able to enlist them to help with the Jihadi effort. The cell's first priority was to modify the attic in The General Store by installing fake partitions at both ends of the building, where contraband would be warehoused for al-Qaeda's later use.

Once the attic project was completed, Hammoud planned to contact Muqtadir to let him know that their arrangement had been finalized, and he was awaiting instructions concerning when to expect the supplies to arrive. He knew Muqtadir would appreciate his cooperation and thank him for his service to al-Qaeda. He hoped that Muqtadir and the al-Qaeda leadership would be very happy that he had fulfilled his solemn obligation to them.

*　　*　　*

Meanwhile back in Grandville, Ashley Khan had been in contact with Muqtadir and informed him that her visit to Palisades Nuclear plant had gone well. The agent had been able to gather similar information, as she had from the Cook Nuclear plant, via the local library and the use of a daily powerboat rental excursion up and down the

Michigan coastline. The land based sides of the nuclear plant were hidden behind dense woods as well, and the agent had been able to enter the woods at night and look at the facility in the early morning hours. Khan assured Muqtadir that no authorities were encountered after embarking on her return trip to the car.

Several hours later, back in the safe house, Khan began to develop the film and compile the observation report. A preliminary evaluation concluded the Palisades facility would be a little easier to access, despite the fact that the Cook facility had been built within the same basic security parameters as Palisades. The agent believed that with the two reactors at Cook to capture, as opposed to one, and the slightly increased security measures at the Cook Nuclear Plant, compared to the Palisades facility, attacking Cook would be worth the extra risk and effort.

Chapter 15

After repeated conversations with his remaining relatives in Tikrit, Najeeb Hammoud was convinced that his mother and brothers were deceased. Out of respect for the loss of his loved ones, Najeeb hosted a special prayer service in remembrance of them at his home. Only his close friends were invited to attend, in their honor. Najeeb understood that death in the Islamic culture was accepted and viewed as a natural part of life, a transition from one state of being to another and not just an end. He believed that his deceased family members had moved on to a pleasant afterlife, separated from the ugliness in the world. With the knowledge of such, he hoped that would help him cope with their loss. Despite Najeeb's understanding, he knew forgiveness for those responsible for their deaths would never be possible. Unless proven otherwise, he would continue to blame the United States and the Shia Muslims in Tikrit for their demise. Under Islamic funeral customs, Najeeb wore dark clothing for the next forty days to remember and respect the passing of his relatives.

A week after the service, Najeeb and his co-

conspirators agreed to begin modifying the space in the attic of The General Store to accommodate al-Qaeda's contraband materials. The store was a two-story structure, rectangular shaped with a sloped roof. It was very similar to an elongated barn. The modifications in the attic involved adding false end walls in front of the existing end walls. With the absence of windows in the attic space, Najeeb knew it would be practically impossible for anyone to ascertain that there were hidden spaces at either end of the structure, unless the original space had been previously recorded or measured. He was doubtful that the specially designed access doors would somehow be discovered. Najeeb also believed it would be highly unlikely anyone would notice their existence, particularly if the attic space was filled with excessive goods and supplies for sale. As a precaution, several shelving units were added both upstairs and downstairs in the retail sales area to explain the nighttime construction noise in the building. It took them several weeks to modify the attic, design and build the doors, and to construct the new shelves before Najeeb was ready to contact Muqtadir.

As Najeeb predicted, Muqtadir was very happy about the modifications they had made in the attic and the fact that they were ready to take al-Qaeda's deliveries. Muqtadir was very hopeful those deliveries would start fairly soon because of the time it would involve to assemble supplies for a mission of this size and scope. Once the supplies were ready to be shipped to the Langdon site, Muqtadir assured Hammoud he would contact him in advance to make sure the newly renovated attic space was completely ready. He also told Hammoud how sorry he was to hear about his relative's demise in Tikrit and asked if there was anything he could personally do to help. Hammoud again briefly wondered how Muqtadir had found out so quickly about their demise, but realized he had many contacts in the Muslim community and that it was not unusual. Hammoud responded there was nothing to be done, but that he appreciated Muqtadir's thoughtful words and condolences.

Within a few days after the attic was finished, Muqtadir proudly sent a message to his United States al-Qaeda superior announcing the existence of an active al-Qaeda sleeper cell in Langdon, Michigan. Several weeks passed before Kazi received his message and communicated back to Muqtadir's United States superior that there was no al-Qaeda action plan, ready or approved to be acted upon, at the present time. However, Kazi stated that the al-Qaeda leadership was very happy to hear of the official's accomplishments and that they were close to resuming their important work in the United States. They encouraged Muqtadir to continue pressing ahead with the establishment of the other five locations.

*   *   *

It was early July in 2003, and Neal Johnson was in his Grand Rapids office reminiscing about his deceased father, James, and his mother, Saarah. James passed away from complications due to a rare form of cancer in February 2002. Neal recalled the many happy memories that his family had experienced in the military. Neal could not forget about the family experiences they shared traveling the globe and the unique variety of duty stations where his Dad had served. He admired how his father had loved and respected his fellow soldiers and the military, despite the problems. Nevertheless, the family had endured some hardships too. James was unable to maintain his security clearance due to excessive debt, a prior bankruptcy, and a foreclosure on a previous home. Without the security clearance, his advancement possibilities were practically null. James had been asked to either accept a new position that did not require a security clearance or retire. He did not like either option, and at one point, he threatened to quit the military. Realizing the possibility that he would never be granted a security clearance again, he decided to retire and informed his superiors of his choice. The military processed his request, and about a year before 9/11, James was honorably discharged and retired, from the Marine Corps.

Shortly after James retired, Saarah Nazir-Johnson, Neal's mother, was beside herself, from the news that her husband had been diagnosed with cancer. Fortunately for the family, James had been granted total disability just prior to his retirement. Saarah blamed the military for his security clearance problems, for his lessor retirement benefits, and for the added stress involved with the uncertainty of his future in the Marine Corps. In addition, she wondered if all the problems James had been experiencing might have contributed to the sudden and unexpected occurrence of cancer.

Months after his death, Saarah seemed to be somewhat

adjusting to her new life as a widow. She sold their home in North Carolina and decided to relocate to Dearborn, Michigan, where some long-time friends of hers were residing. Besides, with her son, Neal, being stationed in Grand Rapids, it made it much easier for her to see him living in Dearborn, than when she lived in Raleigh.

Saarah appeared to be enjoying her new life in Michigan. There were plenty of things for a healthy, intelligent, and active person to do. After much thought, she decided to concentrate on finding a part-time job somewhere within the Islamic community to occupy her spare time. Several months after moving to Dearborn, Saarah went to work for the Muslim Family & Legal Assistance Services organization, headquartered in downtown Detroit. Through her job, she met both domestic and foreign born Muslims. Eventually, she became close friends with several of the foreign born Muslims with whom she worked. In spite of her part-time job commitments, Saarah still had ample time to visit her only child, Neal, in Grand Rapids.

*   *   *

Months after Giordano and Johnson had completed their investigation at Grand Mere state park, Giordano informed his superior, Murrell, they were still continuing to keep track of the case. Fortunately, their on-going investigations back in the Grand Rapids area had gotten a bit more interesting. Giordano had identified several individuals that had made statements he found concerning. Giordano decided to conduct a surveillance probe on all three of those individuals.

The first was Jalal Hafeez, a recent immigrant from Mogadishu, Somalia, who was working at the airport as a baggage handler. He stated he had worked for a local airline in Somalia. But, when Homeland Security was contacted to check him out, they discovered he had not previously worked at an airport. Giordano was concerned he might have other intentions while working at the Gerald R. Ford International Airport terminal in Grand Rapids. Therefore, they began to follow Hafeez to determine where he was going, both before and after work. After several weeks of surveillance, they concluded that he was harmless. He had a wife and a newborn son, and he would come and go from his residence to the airport and back, on a regular schedule. Only occasionally would he change the routine and go to the pharmacy or the grocery store. Daily he would pray at the local mosque before heading off to work. Giordano informed the airport officials of their findings about Hafeez, but nevertheless, still encouraged the authorities to keep an eye on him. They decided it was doubtful Hafeez was a threat, but Giordano thought it would be better to be safe than sorry. Giordano filed a report to Murrell concerning their observations and recommendations.

The second man Giordano had his sights on was, Omar Wahab, a single man, living a quiet existence in rural Grand Rapids. In the interview Johnson and Giordano conducted with him, Wahab stated that he was a widower and that his wife had died several years before. He attended a mosque daily to pray and appeared to have few friends or acquaintances. According to the local police records, it was apparent that he had a long-time drinking problem. When asked about whether or not he had ever had problems with the police, he stated he had not. However, his record indicated otherwise. He had been arrested several times for public intoxication and civil disturbances. Giordano found out Wahab's wife had left him and was not deceased. He had never been involved in anything more serious and had never spent any time in jail. They decided he was not a threat and filed a detailed report to Murrell.

Tazeem Khalid, the third individual, was a different matter. Outwardly he looked like a model citizen; be that as it may, he had associated with some questionable characters in the past. He was employed in one of the local factories as a machinist, but he had been associated with a small group of criminals, known for committing multiple burglaries. When asked about his activities with the group, he denied any involvement. His record indicated otherwise. Khalid had been arrested several times for burglary and was incarcerated twice in the county jail for those crimes. However, he was never convicted and was released due to technicalities. He claimed that, as of lately, he was spending more time with his family and rarely went out. Giordano followed him for three weeks to verify his claim. Their surveillance revealed he had been occasionally meeting with several of his former associates, but to date had not broken the law. Giordano decided to keep him on their watch list and reported the same to Murrell.

Half of their investigations into the more questionable individuals of the Grand Rapids Muslim community had been completed. Thus far, their investigations over several months had developed nothing more than a few persons involved in petty crimes and other minor criminal infractions. Giordano realized that he should be happy they had not uncovered too many sinister characters. Although, finding only a couple subjects with tainted pasts did not allow him much to go on.

Frequently, he wondered if the investigation into his partner, Neal Johnson, would produce any results at all. Perhaps the Bureau, with its newly found "powers" to profile Muslims, was doing just that with Johnson, due to his ancestral background and his employment with the Bureau. Maybe they had no evidence and were just being overly cautious, considering he was a newly released field agent. He was skeptical whether or not the FBI would ever share that information with him. Over time, he believed Johnson would be cleared, and no one would ever know about the investigation, except several FBI executives and himself.

Chapter 16

It was late Friday afternoon, and Abdul Muqtadir was out running errands. When he arrived at his office to drop off some mail, he noticed there was a message waiting for him on the answering machine. The message was only several words long and the caller stated the following, "Approval given for recent order. Best regards, Hastings." Upon listening to the message, he instantly understood its meaning.

Muqtadir was very happy to receive this message. It meant the proposed al-Qaeda plan to overtake the Cook Nuclear Plant, and the attempt to detonate its reactors, was being activated. Hastings was his stateside contact and the go between for al-Qaeda. They had never met before, but Muqtadir received all his instructions through him. Quickly, he sent a message back to him, requesting instructions on how he was to proceed.

*   *   *

The following Monday morning, on the top floor of an old and obscure warehouse space, two blocks from the East River in Brooklyn, New York, sat Mohammed al-Harbia, also known as "Hastings" to his al-Qaeda contacts in the United States and to several others abroad. He was at his desk listening to a cassette tape containing his clandestine phone messages. Those messages were recorded on a remote answering machine that was housed at another location. For security reasons, twice a week on Sunday and Wednesday, he would visit the site and retrieve the cassette tape in the answering machine and exchange it with a new one. Also, it was al-Harbia's standard operating procedure to rent another site every six months and get a new telephone number too. It was a simple way to ensure that his incoming al-Qaeda telephone calls were secure. All outgoing calls for things associated with al-Qaeda business were placed via pay phones.

Muqtadir had called al-Harbia sounding very pleased to have received his message and informed him he was awaiting instructions. In front of him was a copy of the detailed plan for the total destruction of the Cook nuclear facility near Stevensville, Michigan. The plan had been recently promulgated by Anwar Hassan and Faarooq Kazi, one of the head al-Qaeda planners. The final approval came from their superior, Jaabir Muhammad. The familiar sound of the noisy freight elevator below, transporting occupants up to the various floors, was normal, but it sometimes startled him. Out of instinct, he quickly closed the written report and was preparing to conceal it if necessary. He waited several minutes before he reopened the report and began to study it again.

Housed in the warehouse space were some of Mohammed al-Harbia's Middle Eastern artwork pieces that were already sold and ready for shipment. However, the warehouse was also being utilized to stockpile various weapons, explosives, and bomb making paraphernalia. In addition to the weaponry, also housed were blank United States identification forms and communications equipment, which were all hidden behind a fake partition in the back of the room. The hidden space was concealed behind large oil paintings on huge canvases that covered the back wall.

The warehouse space is being leased by al-Harbia's company, MAH Artwork. Al-Harbia appeared to be a legitimate art dealer living in the New York City area, selling original paintings out of his gallery that reflected the traditional Arab lifestyle. Although, his real purpose and mission in the New York City area was to be the intermediary and direct supervisor over all the al-Qaeda affiliates. Like Abdul Muqtadir, he too wanted to be engaged in coordinating terrorist activities in the United States.

Al-Harbia was born in Saudi Arabia and immigrated to the States with his parents at the age of ten. After graduating high school, he traveled back to Saudi Arabia to attend a Madrassa (an institute of higher education) that taught the principles of Wahhabism, a particularly austere and rigid form of Islam. After five years of living in the States, the al-Harbia family had become naturalized American citizens. Despite his parents never being fully radicalized, Mohammad became extremely radicalized not long after he returned from Saudi Arabia. Over the last few years, he had caught the attention of some influential al-Qaeda supporters, who had helped him attain his current status within the hierarchy of al-Qaeda. The legitimacy of his enterprise, and the ability to ship and receive artwork and other articles from around the world, made him a good candidate for undertaking and directing covert activities.

Al-Qaeda had trained him extensively for the position and he had proven to be elusive, intelligent, lethal, and very capable of handling the challenges and responsibilities of the job. He had stayed under the radar and conducted himself skillfully and professionally as a legitimate art dealer. Al-Harbia was a recognized genius with an IQ of over 150 and with his business/management degree; he was more than suitable for managing al-Qaeda projects.

His Manhattan gallery near 5th and East 12th Street was known throughout the New York City area and in other large Muslim communities throughout the United States. Al-Harbia had some very wealthy Muslim clients, like the Khalid's from Saudi Arabia, who occasionally traveled to their Connecticut mansion to indulge themselves in all the finer things New York City had to offer. The Khalid's provided plenty of cash to al-Harbia over the last several years through their purchases of fine art. In addition, they had been able to funnel large sums of illegal cash to support al-Qaeda's activities. Just like Muqtadir, al-Harbia avoided capture following the 9/11 attacks, because his involvement and participation in the al-Qaeda activities were all done clandestinely.

Al-Harbia was intrigued and inspired as he reviewed

the intricate plan, which called for a well-trained team of at least twenty fighters to infiltrate and overtake the Cook facility by force. The team would conduct a series of small surprise attacks on the facility, in the early morning hours. Following the attacks, it was formulated that they would promptly gain access to the reactors and quickly set-off a nuclear explosion. The terrorist plot was designed to kill and maim countless Americans in a fifty-mile radius from the facility. Al-Harbia was instructed to coordinate, compile, and provide most of the materials needed to fulfill the mission through Muqtadir. Other al-Qaeda leaders in the organization would be responsible for the specialized training of the fighters and help get them into the United States via Canada.

*   *   *

That afternoon, Giordano and Johnson returned to the Grand Rapids FBI Headquarters, from an interview with a local Muslim business owner. The man who reportedly had been identified as having been involved in suspicious activity gave them a general tour of his warehouse facility. Giordano and Johnson were there to check things out under the guise of needing some additional storage space for their fictitious business. Things seemed to be in order and the man was well-versed in how to operate a successful business. The inspection of the space had gone well, and they both were convinced the owner was not operating a criminal enterprise to be used by a terrorist organization like al-Qaeda.

It was a rainy day in Grand Rapids, and Giordano closed his eyes briefly while sitting at his desk pondering the many questions that occasionally haunted him. *He couldn't forget about the park ranger's death and the suspicious nature of the incident at Grand Mere State Park. What was the intent of the ranger's murderer? Had he been a foreign agent sent to compile information on the Cook facility? Did the ranger surprise him knowing what the agent was doing in the park? Or, was it an isolated and unrelated criminal incident that had occurred adjacent to the nuclear power plant? Giordano wished there were more clues, but unfortunately, there were not. If only he could figure out the reason for the ranger's death, he knew he could answer more of those questions.*

Johnson came back into the office and saw that Giordano's eyes were closed. "Boss, didn't you get enough sleep last night?" he asked, very tentatively.

"I got plenty of sleep," barked Giordano. "I was just sitting here trying to imagine what might have happened to our deceased Grand Mere park ranger. I keep drawing a blank. I still believe it has something to do with the Cook facility, but I can't prove it."

"Well, maybe we will get lucky and uncover some new evidence sooner rather than later," said Johnson.

"Yeah, maybe we will," said Giordano, sounding surprisingly optimistic and a bit irritated.

Chapter 17

Early Thursday afternoon, after mid-day prayers, the telephone rang in Najeeb Hammoud's office. Hammoud picked up the receiver and said, "General Store, this is Najeeb."

The caller hesitated for a second or two and then responded, "Yusef Foods calling, I have your order ready for delivery today. Are you ready for it, or would you like me to reschedule the delivery?"

Hammoud immediately recognized the raspy voice of Abdul Muqtadir and responded, "I'm getting short on several items. You can deliver them either this afternoon or tomorrow morning. You decide."

"Our truck can be there at 5:30 p.m. today."

"Sounds good," said Hammoud. "Business has been good lately, thanks to Allah's blessings," he stated.

"Glad to hear that," said Muqtadir. "Thank you for the business."

"I will call if I need anything else."

"That will be fine. Thank you again," Muqtadir stated.

*   *   *

Approximately one hundred fifty-five miles south of Langdon, Michigan, in a northern suburb of Indianapolis, Indiana, a bank robbery has just occurred. An off-duty Marion County police officer was seriously wounded in a gun battle, as the two thieves were fleeing out the back door of the bank. One of the robbers was armed with a shotgun and the other with a revolver. The robbers managed to escape with several garbage bags full of cash. In the process, one of the robbers had been shot by an off-duty Sheriff's deputy, as they left the bank. In the chaos that ensued following the robbery, the wounded thief, holding the shotgun, dropped his weapon just before exiting the building. By the time the local police had arrived at the crime scene, the only things left were the wounded deputy, and several frightened bank employees and customers. During the investigation, police took note of: tire tracks in the lawn, drops of the wounded thief's blood, several spent shell casings, and a partially loaded shotgun. There were several witnesses, but the men wore masks and gloves, which made it almost impossible for their race or facial characteristics to be ascertained. However, one of the witnesses speculated that the robbers were Caucasian based on how they walked and the sound of their voices. The bank video security camera system had recorded the event, but the picture was not very clear and the sound was muted.

Several hours later, the local Indianapolis FBI office was brought into the investigation. The authorities were surprised at the fact that, no witnesses had seen the men enter the bank prior to the robbery. Neither the getaway car nor its license plate were noticed by anyone either. The bank heist had only taken several minutes to execute, and it was evident the robbers were very experienced. Because they wore gloves, the authorities were unable to pick up any fingerprints. Without prints, or any physical descriptions of the robbers, knowing the robber's blood type and DNA would not be instantly helpful. The getaway car had made a tire track mark in the sprinkled lawn as it quickly sped through to an adjacent side street exit. The Bureau was busy at the local police laboratory, checking the molds made from the tire marks to help determine the make or model of the getaway vehicle.

The 12-gauge Winchester shotgun that had been left at the crime scene was also being inspected. Although the serial numbers on the gun had been partially ground down, the FBI technicians thought they may still be able to make them out. They were hopeful that if the numbers were legible, they could contact the manufacture and determine who had originally purchased the weapon. They were fairly certain the gun had been stolen at some point after the sale. However, if they knew who the original purchaser was, the information might be able to help them identify the robbery suspects.

On the prior afternoon, in preparation for Friday and Saturdays cash needs, the manager of the bank had ordered a substantial amount of money to be on hand, and the thieves had taken a sizable amount of it. Several days after the robbery, a suspicious car with an Indiana license plate was found by the Michigan State Police, abandoned in a desolate wooded area near New Buffalo, Michigan. It was immediately determined to be the getaway car involved in the Indianapolis area bank robbery. Masks, gloves, and several garbage bags containing loose hundred dollar bills had been found in the back seat. The vehicle had been wiped clean of fingerprints, but there was some DNA evidence remaining inside, which included, dried blood, hair follicles, used bandages, and skin samples. The FBI was able to determine that at least one of the criminals was white, from the evidence left in the vehicle. The authorities believed that there were three people in the getaway car. Several days after the robbery, there was still a hint of cheap smelling perfume lingering in the vehicle. In addition, the investigators found several long strands of blonde hair, full of hair spray, in the driver's seat. This led the authorities to believe the driver must have been a woman.

*　　*　　*

At 4:30 p.m., Hammoud telephoned his three co-conspirators and told them that a special shipment would be arriving at The General Store that evening in an hour. In spite of the short notice given, Hammoud expected his three co-conspirators would all be there to help unload the shipments from Muqtadir's truck. Once the wooden crates were taken up to the attic area, Hammoud assured the men they would no longer be needed and could go home. He planned to go through the items individually himself and store them in the newly concealed attic spaces.

Those spaces had been specifically designed by Hammoud to store military equipment, weapons, ammunition, and miscellaneous gear. Muqtadir had given Hammoud an approximate idea of the scope and size of the spaces needed to store the typical operational shipments. He was amazed that Muqtadir had been able to acquire and ship those things so quickly to him.

Once the shipment had been inventoried and stored away, Hammoud planned to send Muqtadir a message that the crates had arrived at their destination and were ready for use. The shipment included twenty-five 9-mm semi-automatic hand guns with sufficient ammunition, holsters, and silencers. Twenty-five Russian made AK-47's with ammunition, and shoulder straps. Twenty-five green camouflage United States Army fatigues (similar to the uniforms worn by the guards at the Cook Nuclear facility), flak jackets, boots, coats, and head coverings. There was an ample amount of C-4 explosives with detonator kits, and a case containing hand grenades. Also, there were a dozen tear gas canisters, gas masks, four radio transmitters, and a half-dozen radio receivers. After the items were inventoried and stored, Hammoud thought, *it seems there is enough military items and equipment here to fight a small battle.*

Al-Qaeda's methods always involved limited knowledge about their operations to the participants involved. Hammoud's men, as per Muqtadir's instructions, were not told of the contents inside the wooden containers, crates, and boxes. It was evident to Hammoud that his men had their own suspicions about the contents based on their size and weight. He knew these men were not stupid. Regardless, he complied with Muqtadir's instructions in spite of his own feelings. He believed it was silly to hide information from the men, who were risking their own lives and were dedicated to helping al-Qaeda too.

*   *   *

The following Monday morning, Tom Murrell received a phone call from the Indianapolis office of the FBI requesting that the Grand Rapids office assist in the investigation of the bank heist. Since the vehicle used in the Indiana robbery had been found in Michigan, along with several hundred dollars from an Indiana bank, the crime was an interstate event and was under the jurisdiction of the FBI. Murrell informed his counter-part in Indianapolis that they would immediately cooperate with their office and begin going over the vehicle left abandoned in New Buffalo, before reporting their findings.

Just before 5:00 p.m., Giordano checked in with Murrell over another matter. Giordano was informed that since they were already working in the southern part of southwest Michigan, he was assigning the Indiana bank robbery investigation to him and Johnson. The following morning Giordano and Johnson drove to New Buffalo to begin their investigation.

Since the Michigan State Police had found the

abandoned vehicle, Giordano and Johnson were told to go to the New Buffalo police garage, where the vehicle was being stored. The state police laboratory technicians had already gone over the car, so Giordano was not interested in checking over their findings. Out of sheer laziness, a trait rarely exhibited by Giordano, he simply reviewed their findings and sent a preliminary report back to the Grand Rapids and Indianapolis FBI offices.

The FBI report noted that the serial numbers on the hundred dollar bills matched those recorded by the Indianapolis area bank. The masks, gloves, bandages, hair follicles, and plastic bags each contained DNA evidence and had been turned over to the FBI via the Michigan State Police technicians. Over the weekend, no one had seen the abandoned vehicle in the woods. The closest neighbors to the site where the car was found were a Michigan couple living in a dilapidated trailer a half-mile away. They said they did not recall hearing or seeing anything out of the ordinary, over the past weekend. Both Giordano and Johnson were not surprised by their response. The people who lived in that area generally did not cooperate with the authorities. Giordano noted that the non-descript, 1997, crème-colored Chevrolet Malibu, that displayed an Indiana license plate, had been stolen the day of the heist from a nearby employee parking lot. The theft had been discovered around midnight after the owner had gotten off his second-shift job at a GM auto-body plant.

Believing they had completed their investigation, Giordano reported to Murrell that he thought there was nothing left to investigate, and would file an official report in several days. Although he was more interested in continuing to pursue the terrorist investigation, Giordano made sure to indicate to Murrell how much he appreciated being given the added responsibility with the bank case.

Chapter 18

It was late July and combatant training was well underway at a concealed al-Qaeda camp, located not far from the Pakistani border in Afghanistan. Experienced fighters, and some new recruits, were there being trained for various missions, under the direction of Faarooq Kazi one of the planners for al-Qaeda's covert activities. Twenty hand-picked fighters were there as well. They were being specifically trained for the Cook mission that would hopefully be the most aggressive plot ever undertaken in the United States. Kazi was optimistic that the plan was going to be even more horrific, destructive, and satisfying to the leaders of al-Qaeda than the Twin Tower attacks in New York City had been in 2001.

The plan was divided into four separate segments, each overseen by different al-Qaeda coordinators. The first segment involved hand-picking and training the twenty combatants for the mission. Second was transporting the fighters from Afghanistan to the United States, via Canada and moving them across the United States/Canadian border. Once the combatants arrived in the United States, they were quartered briefly prior to the attack at the Cook Nuclear facility. Third was to compile and store military weapons and equipment not far from the Cook plant, to be used in the assault. Fourth was to deliver the weapons and equipment to the fighters, provide a safe house for the twenty-man team to train near Cook, and provide two large panel vans, for transportation. The team leader and the backup were well prepared to communicate, review, and coordinate the specifics about the attack to the combatants.

Kazi was in charge of supervising the training for the team members concerning all the facets needed to fulfill their assignment at Cook. The men had no idea when or where the attack would occur but were told the mission would be to destroy an important facility. The operation would be a suicide mission; this was also something the men needed to be prepared for. During the training, the participants were being heavily indoctrinated on the importance of their assignment to al-Qaeda, and Islam. An experienced Imam, familiar with preparing participants for suicide missions, continued to communicate to the fighters, on a daily basis, on how they and their families would be rewarded by Allah for their sacrifices. They were also told how their immediate families would receive cash payments for their loved-ones, after becoming martyrs for Islam.

The Imam would lead them in their daily prayers. Hopefully, by the time the mission was to occur, they would be spiritually ready to give up their lives for Allah. Also, equally appealing for a suicide combatant was the promise of a special reward of 72 virgins during their afterlife.

Each fighter was being cross-trained to do many of the requirements for the mission, but some were going to be trained for the more specialized aspects. Of course, being able to shoot a semi-automatic hand gun or semi-automatic AK-47 rifle expertly was the first priority for all combatants. All trainees were also instructed on how to throw a hand grenade proficiently. Only a handful of men were being trained on how to use C-4 explosives with detonator kits, pick heavy duty locks, and disable alarm systems and telephone lines. The men were also being trained on the basics of permanently disabling electrical, and natural gas generating systems.

Al Harbia's counter-part in Canada was responsible for making arrangements to pick up the team once they arrived in Canada and to transport them across the border by bus via the Mackinac Bridge. Once in the United States, Muqtadir had a bus driver in Cheboygan, Michigan, ready to meet the team and shuttle them to a prearranged safe house, close to the Cook Nuclear facility.

Hammoud was responsible for storage of the needed military equipment and supplies for the attack. Muqtadir was responsible for providing a safe place where the team members could stay and prepare themselves, prior to the mission. Muqtadir had assigned Ashley Khan, to find and secure a warehouse where they would briefly stay. She had no idea that the fighter's assignments at the Cook facility were part of a suicide mission. She was under the impression that the mission was only to overtake the facility and hold hostages for ransom. Khan also had no idea the scope and range of damage the destruction of the reactors would cause. She was purposely misled concerning the real intent of the operation.

Muqtadir's main functions were to deliver the military weapons, equipment, and supplies to the safe house, provide two vans to transport the men to Cook, and to go over the plan with the al-Qaeda combatant's team leaders. The strategy called for Muqtadir to leave the area a day before the attack and return to his Dearborn home. However, he was to continue communication with the team leaders, up until several hours before the attack was scheduled to begin. He planned to call al-Harbia immediately upon his return to Dearborn and report on the status of the mission,

Muqtadir had been instructed by al-Harbia to leave the area for his own safety and go home, due to the extreme damage the explosion of the reactors was going to create. The al-Qaeda leadership was hopeful that the blast would initially kill, injure, and infect countless Americans with radioactive material. Getting Muqtadir out of the blast area was extremely important to al-Harbia and al-Qaeda. His skills and contacts would be needed for their next mission. Muqtadir was thankful he was more important to al-Qaeda alive than dead.

*   *   *

It was Wednesday afternoon at the downtown Greyhound bus station in Grand Rapids. Khan was waiting to board the next bus to the Dearborn Amtrak train station. She had at least a half-hour to wait, so she decided to call

Muqtadir in Dearborn to check-in. Finding an empty phone booth at the far end of the station, she dialed Muqtadir's number. After a few seconds, he answered the call. "Sales department, Abdul speaking."

"It's me; I'm still in Grand Rapids waiting on a bus."

"I thought you went home yesterday," he said.

"No, I decided to wait to finish my report. I wanted to email it to you before I left. It's the estimated number of customers (code word for the number of police officers) within a twenty-mile radius of the target (code word for the Cook Nuclear facility). I hope you find it helpful."

"Thank you. I will check my computer later today," he said.

"Can you stay in Grand Rapids another night?"

"Yes. Why?" she asked.

"I have a new client (code word for assignment) that I need you to work on. I will email you with the details in a couple of hours."

"I'll be happy to work with your new client." Khan said. "When do you want me to start?"

"Next week will be soon enough. Enjoy the weekend, and I will talk to you later."

With that, Khan hung up the phone.

* * *

The following morning Khan turned on her computer and opened up the e-mail from Muqtadir. To her surprise, the new assignment was to search for an out of the way 10,000-25,000 square foot commercial storage property to lease. The property needed to be located in the vicinity of Stevensville or in the Bridgman area and within a thirty-mile radius of Cook. Muqtadir stated, he did not think it would be too hard to find a place, since there was always a large selection of commercial property for lease on the market in that area.

Khan found Muqtadir's next instructions peculiar. He told her to pick out any Grand Rapids/Kalamazoo/Battle Creek manufacturing firm and find out the Chief Executive Officer's (CEO) name and his secretary's name. Then she was to select a commercial real estate agent to assist her in finding them an available storage facility to lease.

He also cautioned Kahn not to make personal visits or have personal contact with the commercial real estate agent and suggested the assignment should be handled via the telephone. After all, he told her that if the real estate agent were ever questioned by the authorities, following the Cook attack, he did not want to make it easy for the authorities to find her. He suggested that Khan tell the agent that her boss was planning to increase production and would need additional storage space in six months or less. Muqtadir also told her to tell the agent that once a property had been selected, the facilities acquisition manager would get involved. Her job was to locate an appropriate storage location and then turn everything over to the facilities manager.

She realized now why Muqtadir wanted her to select a manufacturing company including the names of the CEO and the CEO's personal secretary. She was going to fictitiously be the CEO's secretary and would be serving as the representative responsible for leasing the property.

In violation of al-Qaeda's rules, Muqtadir had decided to tell Kahn that the Cook project had been approved and that the acquisition of the storage space was an integral part of the plan. Muqtadir highly trusted her, due to her current and past commitments to al-Qaeda. He also felt confident due to the actions she had recently taken for him and for the other radical Islamist movements in the past.

He also reminded her that he would be giving her notice several days before the attack is to take place. He told her that once she received notification she was to vacate the safe house and make sure it was completely sanitized prior to her departure. After the attack, he told her to stay home until instructed to do otherwise. She was also told to memorize the information in the current email and destroy it, as soon as possible.

Chapter 19

It had been several weeks since the Winchester shotgun, which had been used in the Indianapolis bank robbery, was shipped to the FBI laboratories for examination. Giordano and Johnson were waiting to hear the results of the examination from their counterparts in Indianapolis. It was 4:30 p.m. in Grand Rapids, and they were almost ready to go home, when Murrell's moderately attractive, spicy, middle-aged secretary walked into Giordano's office with a manila envelope. "Good afternoon Frank," she said, as she handed him the envelope and openly flirted with him as she always did. "Have you been waiting for this?" she asked, smiling and making it unclear whether she was talking about herself or the envelope.

Frank looked up upon her arrival, but he had already been alerted to her impending appearance by the clapping sound of her high heels coming down the hallway. He always enjoyed the wonderful aroma of her expensive perfume that permeated throughout the office and lingered long after her departure. He had thought about her lustfully on more than one occasion, but reminded himself that he had a loving, faithful, and very attractive wife waiting for him at home. "Thank you for the envelope Adrianna," he said, smiling back at her.

"You're welcome Frank, anytime," she said, as she slowly turned with the skill and grace of a ballerina and strolled out of the office.

"I think she likes you Frank," commented Johnson, after she had left. "Is she always like that to you?"

"I guess so," said Giordano, acting slightly embarrassed. "I still have it. So what?" he said, somewhat jokingly. "It's probably just an act. I think she's really shy." However, he slyly or maybe hopefully thought he knew otherwise.

"I'm not so sure about her shyness," said Johnson. "Let's take a look inside the envelope, shall we Casanova," he said, teasingly to Giordano.

"Good idea," said Giordano, trying to change the subject quickly. "Let's see what the laboratory technicians have to say."

Giordano opened the envelope and began to read the two-page report that had been addressed to the Indianapolis office. To his delight, the FBI technicians reported that they had been able to decipher the serial number on the shotgun, even though it appeared to have been scratched over, probably with a small file. Giordano knew the Indianapolis agents probably had already contacted Winchester to determine the name of the retailer, who had originally purchased the gun for resale.

To Giordano's disbelief, the Indianapolis office was requesting their help in contacting The General Store, the original purchaser of the shotgun, located in Langdon, Michigan. They wanted the Michigan office to try to determine who had purchased the shotgun from the retailer. The second-page was a copy of the original invoice from Winchester to Roger Fleming, the proprietor of The General Store located at 601 South Main Street in Langdon. The Indianapolis FBI office was requesting a complete report from the Grand Rapids office, as soon as possible. "I guess we're back on the bank robbery case," commented Giordano to Johnson. "It's hard to imagine the shotgun involved in the crime was from Langdon," he said, as he was rereading the documents.

After pondering the unlikely probability that the gun was from Langdon, Johnson said, "I wouldn't be surprised if the robbery suspects were from somewhere in southwest Michigan. Indianapolis is not that far away."

"If so, I hope we can get lucky, find the suspects, and maybe solve the case," said Giordano.

Chapter 20

It was a beautiful sunny day in Dearborn, when Saarah awoke and got out of bed. After breakfast, and several cups of coffee, she decided to call her son Neal, who she has not seen or spoken to in over a month. She wanted to see if they could get together in Grand Rapids for the weekend. She picked up the phone and dialed his work number. After several rings he answered, "Agent Johnson speaking."

She responded, "Hi Neal, it's Mom. Can you talk?"

"Hi, I was just thinking about you. Are you at work?"

"No, I'm at home. Work has been pretty slow lately; not quite sure why though," she said. "It's like that sometimes."

"What's up?" asked Neal.

"I'm thinking of coming to Grand Rapids to see you tomorrow. Do you have plans?"

"No, I have the weekend off, thankfully. Things have been very hectic around here lately. I could use a break. What time are you planning to get here?"

"Early Saturday afternoon. Can you pick me up at the downtown Greyhound bus station? I'll call when I get in."

"Sure, I'll come get you," said Neal.

"I'm looking forward to seeing you. How long will you be staying?"

"Unfortunately, just for the weekend. I've got a project to do starting the following week. Therefore, I need to be back in Dearborn by late Monday afternoon. We'll have a nice visit anyway. I'm looking forward to seeing you too," she said. "I know how busy you are so I'll let you go. See you tomorrow, Neal."

"Goodbye Mom," he said, as he hung up the phone.

*   *   *

It was late Friday afternoon and Giordano was preparing to make his weekly call to his former division chief in Washington, D.C. The purpose of the call was to receive his instructions and to give an informal weekly oral report concerning the Johnson investigation. For the past several months, ever since he had begun monitoring Johnson's activities, Giordano had not noticed anything suspicious he could report. However, he thought something must have prompted his former division head to begin the investigation. In an attempt to discover the reason for the probe, Giordano decided he would inquire about the FBI's actions. He thought, *what is the worst thing he could do; tell me it's none of my business or send me to Grand*

144

Rapids, Michigan, as my punishment? As the conversation with his former division head was wrapping up, Giordano stated, "Since I am involved in the investigation, I think I should be entitled to know about Johnson," he said, very cautiously.

"If I were to tell you anything about the Johnson case, it would be a highly unorthodox and unethical thing for me to do, but this investigation is not what I would consider normal or routine," he said. "However, let me preference my comments with this note of confidence in you. I have always thought you were a very fine agent, who somehow got caught up in a political scheme that went terribly wrong. We now know you took the blame for another agent's problem, paid the price, and have been unfairly treated. I am sorry you were put through some very troubling times. I know you still don't quite understand what happened to you, but thankfully you stayed in the Bureau. Please be aware that I personally appreciate the fact that you stayed. I can assure you that those past sacrifices, and your current efforts, will be rewarded in the future."

"I appreciate your praise and compliments on my behalf," said Giordano. "Thank you, but I think I have a right to know what I am dealing with here." stated Giordano once again.

"Well, maybe you do. However, there is some specific information about this case that I cannot completely divulge to you concerning espionage inside the Bureau. Currently, there are some things that we are concerned about, which may or may not involve Johnson. The CIA has an operative close to Osama bin Laden that overheard a conversation by several of the al-Qaeda leaders. The conversation was concerning the formation of special investigative units being formed by all the FBI offices in the United States to specifically profile Muslims. This is in reference to what your supervisor, Special Agent Murrell, has instructed you to do regarding profiling Muslims out of the Grand Rapids office. The problem is your FBI office was the only office purposely given such an instruction. In essence, we've set-up a trap designed to catch a double agent in the Bureau, who has been passing confidential information on to al-Qaeda."

"Really? I understand now why you are so concerned," said Giordano.

"There is more. As far as we know, there are only four people in your office who know specifically about the formation of your special unit. They are Murrell, his secretary Adrianna, Johnson, and yourself. Unbeknownst to you, Adrianna, Murrell, and you have already been cleared by the Bureau. However, Johnson has not. That is why we instructed you to help us monitor his activities, while at work. We have three surveillance teams working around the clock to track his off-duty activities. Thankfully, we have not found him to be involved in any wrong doing, as of yet. But, until he is fully cleared, we are treating him as though he were a double agent, working for them and us."

"I understand your reasoning," said Giordano. "Is there anything more I can do to help?" he asked.

"Not at this time, but I will keep you posted. In the

meantime, continue doing what you are doing."

"Thanks for telling me what's going on and for your trust and confidence in me," said Giordano frankly. "I'll do whatever it takes, but I'd be very shocked if Johnson were a double agent."

"Well, that's what we hope to find out, and fairly quickly," said the division chief, prior to ending their conversation.

Chapter 21

Around noon on Saturday, Saarah Nazir-Johnson, Neal's mother, arrived at the downtown Greyhound Bus Station in Grand Rapids. She departed the bus, collected her bag, and made her way inside the terminal to the nearest pay phone. She called her son's phone number and after a half dozen rings, was disappointed that he failed to answer. A few minutes later, she looked up and to her surprise, saw him coming towards her through the main entrance doorway. He waved and hurried to greet her. "Hi Mom," he said, giving her a hug and kiss on the cheek. "Let me help you with the bag."

"Hi Neal," she said. "I thought I was supposed to call you when I arrived."

"You were, but I picked up the bus schedule the other day, and thought I would surprise you."

"Well, you did."

"Have you had lunch yet?"

"No, but I'd love too," she said. "I'm hungry."

"Alright, let's put your bag in the car first. There's a new eatery not far from here that has great sandwiches. Does that sound alright?" he asked.

"Sure, anything sounds fine," Saarah responded.

"It's not far from here, so if you don't mind, I'd like to walk rather than mess with the car. We can be there in less than five minutes."

"After being crammed in that bus for several hours, a short walk would be good," she said. "I can use the exercise."

"Okay, let's go," he said, as they walked several blocks through downtown Grand Rapids. When they arrived at the restaurant, Neal pointed up to the old facade near the top of the building. "This structure has been here since 1855," he said. "The owners have completely restored the inside. I eat here occasionally for lunch."

"It looks nice," she said.

They entered the restaurant and were quickly seated at a booth, not far from the front door. A server arrived at their table several minutes later with a couple of waters and menus. "I'll give you a little time to decide what looks good," he said, "then I'll be back to take your orders."

"Thanks," said Neal. A few minutes later, the server returned and they both ordered a cheeseburger basket with sweet potato fries, coleslaw, and iced tea. Before the food arrived, Neal asked his mother about her job and if she was still enjoying life in Dearborn.

Saarah responded, "I like my job, because I enjoy

helping people. I've met some new friends and I like living in Dearborn. It's not like living on the East Coast, but that's alright. I was surprised to find I don't miss the slower pace of the Carolinas'. But, enough about me, she stated. How do you like your new job and Grand Rapids?"

"I like my job. I have a great partner and I like Grand Rapids. I've found an upscale apartment in a good neighborhood. It's close to parks, shopping, and entertainment. Ever since I arrived, the Bureau has kept me pretty busy."

"Tell me what sort of things you do for the FBI," she asked.

"Well Mom, I'm really not supposed to discuss the things I do for the federal government with anyone else."

"If you can't trust your Mother, who can you trust?" she asked.

"I guess you have a point. How about I talk in generalities, okay?" he proposed.

"Sure, you don't need to tell me specifics."

"Remember, you can't talk about this stuff with anyone. Agreed?" he said softly.

"Yes, agreed," she said.

"For the last several months, my partner and I have been tasked with investigating the potential for terrorist activity in southwest Michigan. Remember several months ago, when I slipped and told you that our office had been assigned, along with many other offices, to investigate and review all Muslim activity in our area?"

"Yes, vaguely I do."

"Well, that is what my partner and I have been busy doing for the last several months."

"Sounds very exciting Neal," she said. "Have you found any terrorists yet?"

"Not at this time, we haven't," Neal stated, nervously. He was getting a little anxious about discussing his assignments, even with his mother. Happily, he looked up and saw the waiter bringing their food. "I hope you are hungry; they give you a lot to eat here," he said, quickly changing the subject.

"Are you saying I can't leave the table until I've finished everything on my plate?" asked his mother, trying to be witty.

"No, just eat what you want," Neal said, trying not to sound too ridiculous.

Meanwhile, outside the restaurant and unbeknownst to Johnson, team B had been following him and his mother since they had left the bus station. They were waiting in an unmarked vehicle across the street, for the pair to emerge from the restaurant. Team B, an elderly couple, were in a non-descript, light colored sedan and were assigned to follow Johnson and record his activities. Johnson's home had been bugged by the Bureau, and the three teams had been rotating their stake-out duties on Johnson, during his off duty hours. To date, he had neither said nor done anything of a suspicious nature. However, it would have been a major problem had the Bureau known he was discussing work with his mother. Talking about one's work, or a specific case, to anyone other than another FBI agent was forbidden and violated the Bureau's rules. Usually, Johnson was alone at his home, so they recorded very few interactions with anyone. He barely used the telephone, other than when he ordered the occasional pizza to be delivered. However, he did have a girlfriend, who he was beginning to spend more and more time with. Saarah, his mother, would be one of the first house guests the team would be listening too and observing, since the operation had been put into place.

Terrorists in the Heartland

Chapter 22

The weather had taken a turn for the worst, and a moderately heavy rain had taken the place of sunshine, from the prior day. Giordano and Johnson were traveling south towards Langdon. Their destination was The General Store, to talk to the current owner, Najeeb Hammoud, who they discovered had purchased the business from Roger Fleming. They hoped that the sales records on the shotgun used in the Indiana robbery, would still be available. Also, they wanted to ensure the firearms license agreement had been handled properly. About forty miles from the Indiana/Michigan state line they turned right onto a smaller Michigan roadway and headed west. Langdon was approximately twenty miles away. When they arrived, they commented to each other that it looked like the typical little Michigan community. There appeared to be nothing of significance to offer a weary traveler. Neither man could come up with any reason between them to visit Langdon, unless a friend or relative lived there. A lone gas station was located at the corner of the roadway, leading directly into town. There were a few government offices and several retail establishments, all local stores, with no chain businesses. After stopping to get directions from a local resident, they pulled up to a whitewashed building that looked more like a barn than a retail store. There was a small sign attached to the building above the entrance. It read in bold, black letters, The General Store.

The agents parked in one of the lined spots, directly in front of the building, and got out of their black SUV. They briefly looked at the somewhat worn and poorly maintained neighborhood location, before going inside. Once inside the store, they noticed there was no one present and the place seemed almost deserted. However, they noted the retail shelving was full of merchandise and food. On the back of the rear wall was an antiquated frozen food cooler that was full of various types of food. On the right side wall, both hunting and fishing equipment were prominently displayed. Several shotguns were locked inside a display case, and the ammunition was stored on another shelf, under the weapons.

They were just about to head outside to look over the outside of the building again, when they heard someone approaching from the back room. They were surprised to see a tall, bearded man, wearing a white robe and a headdress, entering the room. The man was obviously a foreigner, probably Muslim, based on his general look and appearance, thought Giordano. "May I help you?" asked the man.

"Perhaps," said Giordano. "We'd like to speak with Najeeb Hammoud. Are you Mr. Hammoud?" he asked, after displaying his FBI credentials.

"I am Najeeb," said Hammoud. "What can I do for you

agents?"

"I'm agent Giordano and this is agent Johnson.

We are investigating a felony. Recently, there was a shotgun used in an Indiana bank robbery. The serial number on the weapon was traced back to your store. Apparently, the prior owner, Mr. Fleming, had purchased it for resale from the manufacturer in 1996."

"I see," said Hammoud. "How can I help?" he asked.

"We were wondering if you had any of the old sales records that may show who had originally purchased the shotgun?" asked Giordano. "Also, we would like to look at your firearms license and the sales contract you executed with Mr. Fleming, please."

"Not a problem agent," Hammoud said. "They are both in my office. Also, do you have the make and model of the shotgun and the serial number as well?" asked Hammoud.

"Yes, we have them."

"Fine," he said. "It will probably take several minutes to find the information you are requesting, but I'll be back as soon as possible."

After reviewing his notes, Giordano said, "The weapon is a 12-gauge, Winchester shotgun, and the serial number is WIN7871435012."

"Thank you for your patience," said Hammoud, after he jotted down the information on a small piece of paper. "I keep very good records. I should be right back," he said. Giordano watched carefully as he quickly exited the space and walked into what they presumed to be the back room of the store. Less than five minutes later, he returned with two file folders and a ledger book. "Here are the items you wanted to see," he said, giving the file folders to Giordano. "I have the name of the person who purchased the shotgun from Mr. Fleming, highlighted in the ledger."

"Great, we'll take a look at your license, contract, and the gun purchaser and be on our way, that is, if we find everything is in order."

"Take your time agent, I have nothing to hide. I think you will find everything is in order," said Hammoud.

"I'm sure we will," said Giordano, thinking it was rather odd and somewhat suspicious that the man had said he had nothing to hide. They had not accused him of anything as of yet, but he had found it necessary to comment about not hiding anything. He wondered if the proprietor did, in fact, have something to hide or was that just a nervous sort of comment. Several minutes later, after he had reviewed the contract, the firearms license, and had noted the name and address of the shotgun purchaser, they thanked Hammoud for his assistance and left the building. Once outside, Giordano asked Johnson, "Did that guy give off any bad vibes to you?"

"I caught his comment about not having anything to hide. I wouldn't have expected him to say that unless he did actually have something to hide."

"I think we need to start looking into Mr. Hammoud's life, sooner rather than later," he said.

"I agree," said Johnson.

*　　*　　*

Giordano and Johnson arrived back at the Grand Rapids FBI building around 2:00 p.m. on Monday. They returned immediately to begin their investigations into the lives of Najeeb Hammoud and James Fairaday. Fairaday was the retail buyer of the 12-gauge Winchester shotgun used in the Indiana bank robbery. They decided to look into Fairaday first, since the Indianapolis office was involved and a deputy sheriff's officer had been shot during the robbery. Not surprisingly, Fairaday had no criminal record and resided in the small, rural farming community of Union Mills, Indiana. He had previously lived near Langdon, when he purchased the shotgun from Fleming. According to the FBI records, he now lives in a small home on the outskirts of Union Mills with his wife of many years. He is 75 years-old and previously had a disabled driving permit, last renewed in 1998.

Giordano decided there was no reason to visit Fairaday in person, due to his advanced age and disabled status. So, he picked up the telephone and called Fairaday to inquire about the 12-gauge shotgun. The telephone rang several times before a soft-spoken old lady answered the call. "Fairaday's," she said.

"Good afternoon, this is agent Frank Giordano calling from the Michigan branch office of the FBI. Is James Fairaday there? I'd like to talk to him," he said.

"Why yes, he is. I'll get him for you," she said.

Through the receiver Giordano could hear the woman

say, "Jim, it's the FBI calling. What could they possibly want with you?"

"I have no idea the male voice stated." A minute later, another soft spoken voice got on the phone, "This is Jim Fairaday speaking. Can I help you with something?" he asked.

"Mr. Fairaday, I'm sorry to bother you, but we are involved in a robbery investigation. It seems a 12-gauge shotgun you own was involved in the robbery. Do you still have the gun?" asked Giordano.

"Is it the 12-gauge Winchester that you are referring to?" he asked.

"Yes it is," stated Giordano. "Are you still in possession of the gun?"

"Unfortunately, I am not. There was a break-in at our home several years ago and the gun was taken during the robbery. I reported it as having been stolen to the LaPorte (Indiana) County Sheriff's Office at the time of the incident. They should be able to verify the information I have given you," he said.

"To your knowledge did they ever catch the person or persons who broke into your home?"

"As far as I know, no one was ever apprehended. Is there anything else I can do for you agent?"

"Were there ever any suspects named in the investigation?"

"I have no idea. I guess you'd have to ask the LaPorte Sheriff's department, sir," he said politely.

"Thank you for your assistance. I'll give them a call," Giordano said.

Several minutes later, Giordano called the LaPorte County Sheriff's Department to verify Fairaday's claim. Not surprisingly, they quickly found the records and substantiated all of Fairaday's statements. About a half-hour later, Giordano prepared a report to the Indianapolis FBI office detailing what he had found out concerning the previous owner of the shotgun. Their investigation ended with Mr. Fairaday and offered no immediate help in finding the robbery suspects. However, the investigation into the 12-gauge Winchester had introduced them to Najeeb Hammoud, a potentially interesting person, due to the fact that he appeared to be a non-assimilating American Muslim. Giordano thought it strange; Hammoud was living in a rural setting and conducting business in the non-traditional Muslim community of Langdon. After all, Langdon was a small Michigan farming community with a mix of mostly white farmers and Mexican migrant workers. After consulting with the local authorities, he learned that Hammoud was not the only Muslim residing in Langdon. Apparently, there were approximately thirty Muslim families also residing there.

Outwardly, Hammoud appeared to be harmless, but there was something about him that seemed to concern Giordano. He could not decide why the man found it necessary to make the comment that he had nothing to hide. *If I give the man a second look, what harm would that do,* he thought. *It's always better to err on the side of caution, regardless if I am discriminating.*

Terrorists in the Heartland

Chapter 23

Early Tuesday, around 8:00 a.m., following his morning prayers, Hammoud walked several blocks to downtown Langdon. He sat down at a bench in front of the pharmacy and appeared to be waiting for something or someone. At about 8:15 a.m., the pay telephone that was attached to the outside of the building began to ring. Immediately, he picked up the receiver and said in Arabic, "Mar-[HA]-ba (meaning hello)." For a few seconds there was no response, but then he heard the voice of Abdul Muqtadir say, "Najeeb."

Hammoud answered immediately by saying, "Na-Am (meaning yes)."

Muqtadir sounded rather disgusted and said to him, "I got your message. What is so important? Why did you use my emergency phone number to contact me?"

In a softer than usual voice he stated, "The FBI was in my store yesterday morning. There were two agents. They wanted to look at my records concerning the sale of the business and they wanted to look at my firearms license."

"Did you show them the records?"

"Yes, I complied with their requests. They also said they were there as part of a felony investigation involving a shotgun used in a bank robbery. They claimed that the shotgun had been sold in 1996 by Roger Fleming, the former owner of The General Store. They gave me the serial number and the make and model of the shotgun, and I provided them with the name of the original purchaser."

"Alright," said Muqtadir. Did they say anything else or want to look around the store?"

"No, they did not thankfully," said Hammoud, who was beginning to sound more relaxed.

"It appears as if it was a routine visit to determine who had purchased the shotgun from Fleming in 1996. How did they treat you?"

"They were polite and respectful," said Hammoud.

"What else happened?" asked Muqtadir.

"Nothing really, but I think they were a little surprised to see me in my Arab attire. After a while, I think they got used to it. Their presence in the store alarmed me, but their actions seemed normal. I believe I related well to them. After I presented the information they requested, they did not stay long. It seemed they felt everything was in order. But, believe me Abdul, they were all business."

"In the future Najeeb, you might consider trying to conform more to the American way of life, by dressing more appropriately for life in a small, rural Michigan community. You are not in Iraq anymore. Frankly, you stick out like a sore thumb, and your garments draw immediate attention to the fact that you are different. I would prefer that you try to look more like you are assimilating somewhat into American society."

"No one has ever had a problem with my clothing before, but I do understand what you mean."

"I would not have a problem with it normally, but things have changed. We are trying very hard not to draw attention to ourselves, or the equipment you're storing upstairs in your attic, for obvious reasons."

"It will not be a problem anymore," said Hammoud. "I'll only wear my traditional clothing for special occasions or when I'm at home."

"I hope it's not too late," commented Muqtadir, sternly. "Did they say or mention they would need to return at some point to talk with you again?"

"No, they did not."

"Good, it sounds to me like you have nothing to worry about, my brother. There is no way they could have been there to investigate the contents of the attic. Nothing seems to be problematic, from what you've said. You worry too much. I told you in the beginning that you would not be in jeopardy by helping us, and you are not. Try to forget about their visit unless they come back to talk to you again. Okay?" said Muqtadir.

"Alright. I suppose you are correct. Sorry I alarmed you by calling your emergency phone number. I will not do it again, unless there is a real problem," he promised. "Thanks for your help Abdul."

"Everything is fine," said Muqtadir. "I'll check in with you early next week to see how you are doing. Goodbye."

Chapter 24

Around noon Tuesday, Ashley Khan took a cab to the public library and selected a reference book entitled, "Who's Who in Michigan." After looking through the book, she selected the CEO of Axis Equipment Corporation, a light machinery manufacturer located at 5569 Jennings Blvd., in Battle Creek, Michigan. She quickly noted his name, Paul Livingston, his company's name, phone number, and the company address on a pad of paper, before leaving the library.

About an hour later, she called Axis Corporation. The phone rang once and an operator immediately answered, "Good afternoon, Axis Corporation. How can I help you?"

"Hi, this is Sharla Pendleton. I'm a sales representative for WMMT, we are a news station in Kalamazoo," said Ashley. "We are planning on doing several stories featuring local businesses in an upcoming manufacturing magazine. I'd like to include highlights of Mr. Livingston's company in the publication. Could I speak to him, please?"

"I'm very sorry, but you'll need to speak with his

secretary first," she said, politely. "Her line is busy right now. Can I put you on hold?"

"No, that won't be necessary. I'll call her back later," said Ashley. "However, if I could have her name please, that would be helpful."

"Sure, her name is Marsha Showalter, but she will probably refer you to the marketing department for your inquiries."

"That's fine, but I'd like to talk to her first," insisted Ashley.

"I'll let her make that decision," the receptionist stated, in a matter-of-factly and almost domineering manner.

"I appreciate your help," said Ashley politely, as she quickly hung up the telephone.

Several minutes later, she called the Stevensville Chamber of Commerce and asked for the name of a highly reputable local real estate agent. Within minutes, she had been given the telephone number of Kay Sanders, a well-known commercial real estate agent with a great reputation and track record.

Later that afternoon, Khan called Sanders to discuss the need for storage space to rent for Axis Equipment Corporation. Sanders operated a small independent commercial real estate firm between Stevensville and Benton Harbor. She had been in business for well over twenty years. The phone rang in her office, and she immediately answered the call. "Kay Sanders speaking," she said.

"Hi Kay, this is Marsha Showalter calling. I'm the executive secretary for Mr. Paul Livingston; he's the CEO of Axis Equipment in Battle Creek."

"Hello Marsha, how can I help you?" she responded in a friendly tone.

"Our company has plans to expand our production capabilities later this year. We need to find a temporary site to warehouse our products for several months until we can begin using the larger space that's currently under construction. Can you help me find a space between 10,000 and 25,000 square feet to rent for October, November, and December 2003?" she asked. "We'd like the storage facility to be located near Stevensville, Michigan. Will that be a problem?"

"No problem at all Marsha. That is one of the many services I provide to my clients. Let me send you a contract and all you will need to do is sign it and return it to me," she said.

"Sounds simple enough," said Khan. "I'll give you my contact information and my personal phone number. You can take it from there. How much time do you think it will take to locate a facility for us to rent?"

"There is plenty of property on the market. As you know, the economy is not the greatest these days. Would you consider a rent/purchase option in case you change your mind about needing it for only three months?" Sanders inquired.

"It's possible. I can discuss it with Mr. Livingston and get back to you," she said.

"That will be fine. I'll wait to hear from you, but in the meantime I will start looking for several suitable locations."

"That would be wonderful. I'll check back with you in a few weeks," said Khan. "Goodbye," she said, as she quickly hung up the phone.

Chapter 25

It was 10:00 p.m. on a Thursday evening, and Johnson and several of the neighbors from his condominium complex had just returned home, from a boy's night out bowling event. Occasionally, the group went out to bowl, attend ball games, or for dinner. At 10:30 p.m. the phone rang and he immediately picked up the receiver. "Hello," he said."

"Hi sweetheart how was your day?" asked the sultry sounding voice.

"Are you back in town?" he asked, in hopes she would say yes.

"No, I'm in Tampa for the night. I was kind of lonely, so I thought I'd try and catch you. Did you go bowling?" asked Latoya.

"I did," said Neil. "I bowled a 185 on my first game and 210 on my second. Not too bad for someone who has not bowled much over the last four years," he said, boasting a little.

"Well, better not quit your day job quite yet," she said

teasingly. "A professional bowler you are not."

"No, not yet," he said. "How many flights did you have today?" he asked, changing the subject quickly.

"More than enough," she said. "I'm tired."

"Where do you go tomorrow?"

"O'Hare first, then Orlando, and I finish back at O'Hare. Not too hectic. I should be back in Grand Rapids before 3:00 p.m. on Friday."

"Want to have dinner Friday evening at Winthrop's and then go bar hopping?" he asked.

"Steaks at Winthrop's and then a quiet evening alone sounds better to me."

"Okay, meet me at the restaurant around 5:30 p.m. and I will be there," he said.

"Sounds great, I'll see you tomorrow night. I love you honey," she said.

"I love you too," said Johnson.

Pausing briefly before hanging up, she said, "I miss you, and I wanted to hear your voice before going to bed. I wish we could talk longer, but I'm really tired tonight for some reason."

"I miss you too, but I understand," he said. "We can talk tomorrow night for hours or do whatever," he said. "I can't wait to see you. I've got a busy day tomorrow and it sounds like you do too. See you tomorrow night."

"That's fine," she said in agreement. We can talk tomorrow night, and after dinner we can go back to your place and relax. Goodnight honey."

"Goodnight sweetheart," he said, as he hung up the phone. He was excited after hearing the probability of her wanting to go back to his place. Johnson knew what relax meant and so did she. It had been almost a week since they had seen each other, and apparently, she was horny too.

Several minutes later, she picked up the phone again and dialed a familiar number. A man answered and Latoya said, "Hey, it's me. I just talked to him a couple of minutes ago. We have a dinner date tomorrow night at Winthrop's Steakhouse in downtown Grand Rapids."

"Where are you?" asked the man.

"At the apartment," she said. "I'm sleeping in my bed tonight, as opposed to the office couch."

"Team C just reported that he arrived home around 10:00 p.m. and is currently in the bedroom watching television."

"I guess he is being honest about his extracurricular activities. I like that in a man," she said. "Under different circumstances, I think I could really start to like him. Too bad I'm on assignment."

"Well, if he checks out, maybe you two could still get together," said her boss.

"I doubt it," she said. "How would I ever explain working undercover for the FBI and he being the subject of my investigation? It would be too complicated."

"Yeah, I guess you're right. Sleep well Miss Smith," he said jokingly. "I'll talk to you tomorrow."

"Okay, goodnight," she said.

Teresa James, a/k/a Latoya Smith, had worked for the FBI for almost four years, prior to this assignment. She was several years older than Johnson, but her age difference did not seem to bother him. She had been in the special operations unit for the past two years. Teresa was a beautiful looking, light-skinned African American, with a shapely figure, and a very bright mind. She had the ability to know exactly what to do to attract men. Normally, she was not expected to be intimate with her contacts, but the Bureau had never questioned her motives or actions. She was an excellent agent, who seemed to be on a fast track to a big promotion at the FBI.

When the opportunity arose for her to work with James Miller, her current supervisor, and a rising superstar in the Bureau, she jumped at the chance. Miller had a reputation for being a solid agent, who always fulfilled his assigned tasks in record speed and with excellent results. He would be a good reference for her to use when the time was right. Miller's job was to supervise the three surveillance teams and Teresa James in their investigation of FBI Agent Neil Johnson.

She had been seeing Johnson for the last couple of months, and she believed he had fallen head over heels in love with her. Once their assignment was completed, regardless of the result, she was going to have a hard time walking away from him without giving an explanation. However, that was the job, and she understood the consequences of her actions. Besides, she had needs too, like anyone, and Johnson had been there at the right time and place. She thought he would be heartbroken in the end.

*   *   *

On Friday afternoon, Giordano and Johnson began their investigation of Najeeb Hammoud. They immediately wanted to look into the Bureau's and the State of Michigan's records for information on Najeeb Hammoud. In addition, they also contacted the Department of Homeland Security (DHS) to have them review the background of Mr. Hammoud, as well as his family. Previously, they would have accessed that information through Customs and Border Patrol (CBP), but on November 25, 2002, President George W. Bush had combined twenty-two different Federal agencies into the DHS, which included the CBP. DHS's mission, following 9/11, was to prevent attacks and protect Americans on land, sea, and air. Bush's action was the largest United States government reorganization in the fifty years since the United States Department of Defense was created.

Giordano wanted to know what country Hammoud had come from and whether or not he still had family living overseas. They wanted to know all about his activities in his home country and what he had been doing since he entered the United States. They also wanted to know if he was a naturalized American citizen, residing in the United States, or was he here on a visa? He informed the clerk at DHS that he wanted to know everything there was to know about Najeeb Hammoud and as soon as possible. In addition, he also contacted Murrell and filled him in on Hammoud.

Just before 5:00 p.m., some of the information Johnson and Giordano had requested about Hammoud began to arrive over their secure line from Washington, D.C. Giordano began reading the partially completed report and found it to be quite extensive. But, he decided it could wait until the following Monday. It had been a long week, and Johnson seemed to be acting like he was in a hurry to go home. Giordano turned off the light, locked the door, and they both departed the building. Prior to leaving, they agreed to come in early on Monday morning.

Chapter 26

Winthrop's Steakhouse in downtown Grand Rapids had a long standing tradition of excellence when it came to fine dining, particularly steak. They specialized in filets, strips, rib eyes, and prime rib. In addition, they are known for their lobster bisque and giant shrimp cocktails. It is the premier restaurant to dine at in downtown Grand Rapids and for the surrounding area too. Johnson loved to eat there in spite of the typically large bill presented after the meal. Generally not affordable on an FBI man's budget, but Johnson thought, occasionally dining there was worth it.

When Latoya entered Winthrop's, he was waiting for her at the bar. She looked stunning, and some of the patrons at the bar turned their heads to get a glimpse of her, as she walked past their stools. She wore a revealing red dress and high heels that accentuated the muscles in her long, lovely legs. To top it off, the fragrance of her perfume was almost mesmerizing. Latoya spotted Johnson sitting near the end of the bar and quickly walked over to him. She gave him an extra-long hug and kiss. "Hi baby," she said. "Have you been waiting long? Traffic from the airport was terrible."

"No, I've only been here a few minutes," he said, telling her a white lie. He had been waiting there since he got off from work at 5:00 p.m. Johnson was so excited to see her he could not help himself. It had been almost a week since they had been together, and when they embraced he knew that it had been too long. He was not upset as he witnessed some of the male patrons, concentrating particularly on her figure, as she passed them by. He knew they were not only looking at her figure, but also were fantasizing about what they might see under her dress. Johnson felt lucky that she had chosen to be with him, instead of someone else.

Johnson himself was also used to being noticed and appreciated, by women. He was a tall, light-skinned African American, with a wonderful smile and physique. In addition, he was highly intelligent, funny, and had a delightful personality, along with a line of bullshit that most women, unconsciously, loved to hear.

After eating a great meal, and being pampered by an excellent serving staff, they decided to go back to Johnson's place, instead of bar hopping. Upon arriving at his apartment, they made themselves a drink and turned on some romantic music. It only took several minutes before they began to passionately hug, kiss, and make love, on top of the bed spread. After an hour of passionate love-making, they fell asleep, locked in each other's arms.

Chapter 27

A few weeks prior to the Cook Nuclear assault, the telephone rang inside the office of the Pine Valley Tree Farm, just outside of Portage, Michigan. The proprietor, James Barrett, answered the phone. "Hello," he said. "Pine Valley Farms, James Barrett speaking."

"Good morning James," answered the voice. "This is Paul Kellogg. I'm the manager of the Fleetwood Mall in Portage. I would like to place an order for six Christmas trees. I understand you deliver."

"Yes we do. How soon do you want them, and I'll need to know what kind of trees and the size you'd like? I assume I'm to deliver them to the Mall?" said Barrett.

"Yes, they will be part of the Christmas decorations inside the building. But, first I'd like to apologize for the short notice."

"No problem at all," said Barrett.

I've heard you were very good and I just decided a few days ago to get the Christmas trees. I'd like them to be six feet tall, full, and Fraser firs, if you have them. Please deliver the trees on Friday, November 28th, to the Mall. I will mail you a diagram of the locations where I want the trees to be placed, along with a check. Probably would be best to deliver them before the Mall opens."

"I think we can make that happen early Friday morning," said Barrett.

"Just see our security guy at the north-end of the building that morning, and he will let you in. Tell him you talked to the Mall manager and that he asked you to place the trees inside the Mall. Show him the diagram that I'll send you. There shouldn't be a problem."

"Okay, that sounds great," said Barrett.

"Perfect. I'll have the speakers sent to your business. Also, I would like the trees to be planted in oversized containers, so the speakers will fit underneath the tree branches on the bottom. How much is this going to cost?" he asked.

"I'll charge you $250 for each tree, the container, and to individually transplant them and $500 for placement and delivery of all the trees. How does that sound?"

"Too high, but I'll take it," said Kellogg. "When you receive the speakers from my vendor, please put one underneath each tree. The speakers are rectangular shaped, about eight inches by ten inches, and are fairly heavy. They should be able to fit under the trees. We will be responsible for hooking them up to our sound system later in the day."

"My men will be there with the trees, as you requested, on Friday. Thanks for your business Mr. Kellogg, and

Merry Christmas," said Barrett.

"If I like your service and trees, I will use you again next year. Merry Christmas to you, as well," said Kellogg.

Terrorists in the Heartland

Chapter 28

On Monday morning, Giordano was pleased to receive Najeeb Hammoud's complete background information he had requested. The report was quite detailed, and he was surprised that the Homeland Security Department had been able to compile such an extensive dossier on the man so quickly. After all, Hammoud appeared to be a law abiding, naturalized American citizen, who had no past history of terrorist activity or wrong-doing on his record. Giordano knew the Bureau could be as efficient and swift as it wanted to be, depending on the circumstances.

The report stated Hammoud was born in Tikrit, Iraq, on August 29, 1967. He was the oldest of three sons born to Mohamed and Kalila Foraq-Hammoud, who raised him in Tikrit. His father, Mohamed, was a shopkeeper, who specialized in selling Persian rugs overseas. He made a good living and taught his eldest son, at an early age, the art of selling products.

In 1980, Iraq and Iran were at war, and the on-going conflict devastated the Iraqi economy for the next eight years. Saddam Hussein had just risen to power officially and was concentrating on growing the military instead of trying to maintain the economy. Hammoud's father tried to keep the business afloat, but the war effort made it practically impossible for him to continue the business. Ultimately, the business closed several years after the start of the war, and Mohamed was forced to join in the war effort, in order to take care of his family. In 1986, he was one of 60,000 prisoners captured by the Iranians. Mohamed was never heard from again.

At the early age of 21, Najeeb decided to leave Iraq and go to the United States in search of business opportunities there. In 1988, when he arrived in the United States from Iraq, he applied for a work permit. Once the permit was approved, he immediately moved to Dearborn. Since he already had Iraqi contacts in the United States Persian rug business, Najeeb naturally tried starting a rug importation business in Dearborn, Michigan. The venture failed, but by that time he had been introduced to some influential Dearborn Iraqi business people, who helped him restart the business. Najeeb had met them at the Mosque where he attended daily prayers. Unbeknownst to the FBI, the Homeland Security Department, and Giordano, the Mosque is where he met his long-time acquaintance, benefactor, an al-Qaeda sympathizer, Abdul Muqtadir, who also helped him get back on his feet financially.

Najeeb became a naturalized United States citizen in 1993, because of his excellent reputation as a good businessman. He also had the help and support of reputable Iraqi contacts in Dearborn, who knew him and attended his Mosque. Once the business grew more successful, Najeeb was able to send much needed money to his mother in Iraq.

According to his bank records in late 1996, Najeeb managed to repay all his debts and acquire a small retail business in Dearborn.

Giordano was impressed to learn that Najeeb had been sending money to support his family, still living in Iraq, almost from the time he entered the United States. He thought it was admirable and understood why the Bureau was portraying Hammoud as someone who was motivated, out of necessity, to make as much money as possible. He compared Najeeb's efforts to his own father's struggles. Giordano's father regularly stated his obligation to the family, believing his solemn duty was to work hard and take care of his four small children and wife during the early 50's. Although, Giordano's father was a second generation immigrant as compared to Hammoud, who was a first generation immigrant, providing for their families was still challenging.

Hammoud sold his small business in Dearborn in 2000 and moved to Langdon. He, his wife, Amira, and their infant child arrived in Langdon just prior to the completion of the sale. Shortly after arriving in town, he purchased The General Store from Roger Fleming, who was retiring. The Homeland Security Department claimed they had carefully reviewed Najeeb's personal information and believed the Sunni Muslim posed no threat to the Country and was not involved in any terrorist activity.

Giordano was relieved, but still not satisfied, that there was nothing there. He was convinced that something of importance was being overlooked by the Bureau, concerning the man's life. *I am still concerned about*

Hammoud's appearance. His clothing and long beard do not seem indicative of someone who is assimilating very well as a United States citizen, Giordano thought to himself. *Or, maybe I am just grasping at straws, trying to find someone to connect with terrorism?*

Chapter 29

Temperatures were in the mid-thirties at the Charles de Gaulle International Airport in Paris, France, for November 23, 2003. The weather was unseasonably cold. The flight from Benazir International airport in Islamabad, Pakistan, to Charles de Gaulle was slightly more than eight hours, and the passengers were more than ready to disembark once the flight landed. The daily Air France flight was always crowed and attracted mostly family and business flyers.

On this late Sunday afternoon, there were also several dozen young, physically fit men, wearing dark coats that were deplaning. They wore sports shirts with small, almost indistinguishable, lettering and blue jeans. The insignia depicted an Olympic logo along with lettering stating the men were members of the Afghanistan National Olympic team. The men were quiet, respectful, and quickly disembarked the plane, along with the other passengers, looking for bathrooms and restaurants inside the terminal. Several hours later, the group boarded another airplane scheduled to fly to Toronto, Canada, and arrive around

10:00 p.m. that Sunday evening.

The group consisted of twenty players and two older coaches, who were definitely in charge of the team. All the men carried the same small, carry-on bags with an Olympic decal printed on each. Once the team arrived in Toronto, they were scheduled to spend the night at a hotel. The following morning, they departed Toronto on a tour bus headed for the 2004 Winter Olympics site in British Columbia. Normally, they would have flown directly to British Columbia, but they were also scheduled for a sight-seeing tour, according to their official paperwork from the Afghanistan Travel Ministry. Unbeknownst to the authorities, Al-Qaeda officials had bribed someone in the Ministry office to provide documentation, authorization, and passports for all the members of the athletic tour group. The bus tour was supposed to travel north and west from Toronto to Sault Ste. Marie. The tour had been arranged by Canadian al-Qaeda affiliates from Toronto. The plan was to transport them to Sault Ste. Marie via charter bus and await there for further instructions, from other United States al-Qaeda affiliates, in Cheboygan, Michigan. Upon entering the United States, they would be transported across the Mackinac Bridge via another charter bus and arrive in southwest Michigan, later that same day. Their ultimate destination, unbeknownst to the group, was for them to arrive and spend several days near the Cook Nuclear plant, where they would ultimately be conducting their assault mission.

Once in Sault Ste. Marie, an associate of Abdul Muqtadir had arranged for them to have the necessary documentation from Canada and visas to enter the United

States. Their travel packet included falsified letters of explanation from both the International Olympics and the United States Olympics committees. Those letters explained their brief visit to Chicago, Illinois, to attend a Chicago Bears football game, as the Bears special guests. The phony documentation from the Bears was also provided by Muqtadir, through a friend who had an acquaintance connected to the Bears marketing department.

Prior to entering the United States, their paperwork was inspected at the United States/Canadian border and was quickly approved by a United States Customs official. The official was happy to cooperate with both the Bears and the United States Olympic committee. The false Chicago Bears marketing representative, who was not a United States citizen himself, arrived at the United States border, along with Muqtadir, to accompany the group. The representative, acting as a goodwill ambassador for the Bears, was very friendly to the border official. He made sure to provide him with four complimentary tickets to a forthcoming Bears/Lions football game in Detroit, after the group had received approval for entry into the United States.

Chapter 30

On the previous Saturday evening, November 22, 2003, two of Muqtadir's men had arrived at The General Store in Langdon, driving large, white step vans. When Muqtadir's men got to the store, Hammoud was there to greet them, along with his three associates. The vans were parked behind the building and the associates quickly began loading the vehicles with the al-Qaeda contraband. They worked as if they were operating in panic mode. It took about fifteen minutes before Hammoud appeared and told the drivers that all the items had been successfully loaded into the vans. Hammoud quickly said goodbye to the men, wished them luck, and the blessings of Allah, for a successful operation.

Unbeknownst to Hammoud, Giordano and Johnson were about a half-hour away from Langdon, in an unmarked vehicle. They planned on setting up a surveillance operation at The General Store to see if they could determine whether Hammoud was involved in any criminal activities. After Giordano had consulted with Murrell, the supervisor approved a limited surveillance operation, based solely on Giordano's instinct and intuition.

*   *   *

It was early Monday morning, November 24, 2003, when the group entered the United States and traveled across the Mackinac Bridge. By mid-morning, the group reached the rental warehouse, near Stevensville, Michigan. Abdul Muqtadir was on the bus and was pleased to see his men had arrived safely at the warehouse. His right hand man waited in one of the step vans, which was labeled "Axis Equipment Corporation, Acquisitions Division," along with the other driver, who was in the second step van.

Once the men and their small bags were unloaded off the bus, the bus driver chatted briefly with Muqtadir, before parking the bus behind the warehouse. Muqtadir quickly directed the men to go inside the warehouse. He remained outside talking to their two supervisors briefly, before opening the overhead door and motioning for his men to park the step vans inside. Almost immediately, the supervisors began barking orders to the men. The vans were to be emptied of their equipment, weapons, ammunition, and food. It took only several minutes before the contents of the vans were completely emptied and organized.

Muqtadir showed them to the bathrooms and the small break room, which included a refrigerator and microwave, on the main floor. In the smaller upstairs portion of the warehouse is where Muqtadir had arranged to set up a temporary sleeping area. Blankets and pillows were stacked inside the room, for the men to use. Muqtadir was sure the lack of bedding or mattresses would be acceptable; he assumed the men generally slept on the cold ground anyway. On Sunday evening, one of the van drivers turned on the heat in the building, so the men were at least warm. They were tired and hungry. They quickly grabbed a pillow and blanket to set up their beds, before going to the break room to get something to eat. Most had never used a microwave before and were dazzled at how quickly food could be heated up in the strange contraption. After lunch, the supervisors instructed them to start rounding up the equipment and uniforms that they would need for the assault.

Downstairs, Muqtadir and the supervisors had taped large posters on the walls inside one of the enclosed rooms. They were discussing the assault and overall planning, as the young saboteurs began entering the room. Once all the men were inside the room, the lead supervisor began to explain the mission to the men. Their mission, he explained, was to attack the Cook Nuclear Facility and to completely destroy the two reactors inside the facility. He reminded them again of the importance of the Jihadi mission to al-Qaeda, and Islam. Both of the supervisors and Muqtadir thanked them, in advance, for their sacrifice for Allah. Following the brief meeting, they were dismissed to say their prayers with the other supervisor, who among other things, was an Imam trained to prepare the combatants for their upcoming suicide mission.

Later in the afternoon, the men were instructed to try on their uniforms and to compile their equipment. Afterwards, the lead supervisor briefed them again on the mission and broke them off into small groups to go over their individual assignments. Muqtadir stayed and studied their assignments with them. Occasionally, he would comment about something, but he mostly allowed the instructors to do what they had been training themselves and their men to do. Before departing for the day, Muqtadir turned over the boxes, holding the small suicide vests, to the instructors that were provided for the combatants to wear. The instructors were there for two purposes. The main purpose was to train and lead the men. The second purpose was to ensure that all the combatants were wearing the vests, during the assault. Whether the mission was successful or not, the supervisors were there to ensure that none of the combatants would survive. That was the reason for the use of the vests. They were ultimately going to be martyrs whether they liked it or not.

Chapter 31

On Tuesday, November 25, 2003, the al-Qaeda combatants got up and continued their training inside the warehouse, under their instructors' supervision. Muqtadir had planned to be involved in the training phase, however, at the direction of Hastings (Mohammed al-Harbia), his stateside al-Qaeda supervisor, Muqtadir was asked only to observe. The charter bus driver had spent the prior evening in a local motel. He was supposed to pick up Muqtadir at the warehouse and leave around 8:00 a.m., to depart back to his northern Michigan home. Muqtadir had left his vehicle at the charter facility, so he would be traveling with the bus driver, to retrieve his car. As Muqtadir explained to the bus driver, his supervisor, Hastings, wanted Muqtadir to debrief him along the way, pay him, and get to know him better for future assignments. Unbeknownst to the bus driver, they did not want him to go unattended for fear that he might have second thoughts about the operation and tell the authorities. In addition, Hastings wanted Muqtadir to put the man at ease, before he killed him.

Around 11:00 a.m., they stopped at a McDonald's for a

sandwich and a drink. It was a long drive, and the bus driver suggested Muqtadir might want to take a little nap. The trip was going to take several more hours before they would arrive back at his facility in the outskirts of Cheboygan, Michigan. Muqtadir told the bus driver, he planned to drive to Dearborn immediately after retrieving his car.

The charter business office was housed inside the bus driver's outbuilding at his rural home. Muqtadir's car was parked inside the building, for security reasons. When they finally arrived back at the charter facility, Muqtadir helped him unload his suitcase and followed the bus driver into the small office. The bus driver seemed relaxed and unconcerned about Muqtadir having traveled home with him. He had a pocketful of money and had high hopes for more lucrative opportunities in the future.

Once inside the office, the bus driver flipped on the lights and asked Muqtadir if he needed to use the restroom, before departing. Muqtadir said yes, and the driver pointed to the open door, near the back of the room. After relieving himself, he verified that his garrote was inside his jacket pocket. He slowly opened the bathroom door, and approached the man from behind. The bus driver was sitting at his desk reviewing some correspondence, as Muqtadir slowly moved towards him. Both men were about the same height, but Muqtadir appeared to be stronger and more muscular than his target. Sensing and hearing Muqtadir from behind him, he said to Muqtadir, without turning around, "How about some food or drink for the road?"

"Sure. What do you have?" responded Muqtadir.

"How about a cold meat sandwich, an apple, and a couple of sodas?" offered the bus operator.

"Sounds good to me," said Muqtadir.

"Give me a minute or two and then I'll go get your food," he said.

"No problem. Take your time. I'll just look around your shop until you return," said Muqtadir, as he quickly appraised the surroundings.

"Not much to see," said the bus driver.

More than enough to see, thought Muqtadir to himself, as he quickly eyeballed the contents on top of the man's desk for any potential weapons. After seeing none, he took the garrote from his pocket and quickly placed it around the man's neck and began to strangle him. The bus driver was completely surprised as Muqtadir tightened the rope around his neck. Upon feeling the garrote, he tried removing it with his hands. The man struggled violently for several minutes, attempting unsuccessfully to dislodge the rope. Muqtadir lifted the man out of the chair, as the garrote cut off the flow of oxygen to his brain. For several minutes the bus driver was suspended off the chair, until he became unconscious and finally died. Muqtadir waited several minutes, before he lowered the body back onto the office chair. Several minutes later, he carried the man's lifeless body towards his car and placed it inside the trunk.

The bus driver's property was located in a secluded, rural location. His thirty-acre lot was large and expansive, full of pine, oak, maple, birch, and aspen trees. There was a small pond, located at the very back of the lot. The bus driver's acreage was home to lots of wildlife, including birds, raccoons, rabbits, squirrels, and deer. Muqtadir drove about a half mile behind the man's house and outbuildings, before he stopped the car. He selected a clearing among the pine trees, where he buried the body. The soil was extremely sandy and Muqtadir had no trouble digging an ample hole, for the corpse. Prior to putting him into the pit, Muqtadir had made sure to take all his money from his pockets. Once the man was rolled into the pit, he quickly filled it up with sand, and departed, as per Hastings instructions.

Hastings had decided to have the man killed, because he subscribed to the theory that, dead men tell no tales. He reasoned that the bus operator was not an important enough player to salvage and was not trustworthy enough to keep his mouth shut. Besides, in case the authorities would ever find him and interview him about the attack, he would not be able to implicate either one of them, concerning the Cook attack.

Hastings and Muqtadir knew he was going to die almost immediately after he was recruited for the work. In fact, that was the main reason he was hired by Muqtadir, because he was deemed disposable. Hastings thought the man, who basically lived like a hermit, was not well-enough known or liked and that he would hardly be missed by anyone. Although the bus driver had no real knowledge of the mission, he had been exposed to the cartons and the foreign combatants that he had transported to the warehouse, from Canada. Hastings was fearful he could someday become a problem. However, the bus driver was motivated by the promise of a job that paid extremely well and for future opportunities. Truth be known, he could have cared less about their mission.

On the previous day, Hastings had questioned Muqtadir about the reliability of Ashley Khan. Unbeknownst to Muqtadir, Hastings did have some knowledge of the family and really had no reason to question Khan, other than it was the smart thing to do. *You can never be too careful in these matters,* thought Hastings. Hastings also inquired about the whereabouts of Khan and was told by Muqtadir that he planned to contact her later that morning in Grand Rapids to tell her to vacate the safe house. He planned to remind her that she needed to thoroughly clean the apartment of DNA, prints, and personal items before departing.

Muqtadir's plans were for Khan to go home after sanitizing the apartment and wait for his call, following the early Thanksgiving morning attack. *He wondered if Hastings would ultimately instruct him to dispose of Khan too. He hoped not, because she had been very helpful in regards to arranging for the warehouse and providing the background information about the nuclear facilities.* However, if Hastings knew that Muqtadir had given her more information about the mission, than would normally be allowed, he would have not been happy. Muqtadir trusted her completely though and was satisfied that she had done an adequate job for them. Her only screw-up was the murder of the park ranger, but she had panicked and the rest was history. Muqtadir was thankful she had not left behind any clues as to the origin or purpose of her visit.

Muqtadir was also thankful that she had not gotten him involved in the murder, and not complicated matters for him or Hastings. If she had been captured and interrogated by the authorities, due to an incompetent error, he could have been implicated in the plot. However, prior to his meeting with Hastings, he had thought about various possible scenarios in regards to her elimination, if deemed necessary. If he were asked to kill her, he wanted to be ready. *Her life in exchange for his was always going to be a better trade,* he thought. Although Muqtadir was not a trained assassin, he had experience in making problems permanently disappear.

At the very least, he anticipated having to debrief her prior to the attack. He prayed the mission would be successful; otherwise, Hastings would be looking to blame someone, other than himself, for its failure. Muqtadir knew there would be praise for success and consequences for a catastrophe. Muqtadir questioned whether or not there were going to be enough combatants to fulfill the mission, but he was not going to second-guess the wisdom and decisions of the al-Qaeda leadership. He thought, *it was evident 9/11had turned out well, and he hoped the Cook Nuclear attack, which would be referred to in the future as 11/27, would also go well.*

*   *   *

Late Tuesday afternoon, three days before the Mall attack, Barrett, the owner of Pine Valley Tree Farm, received a call from Paul Kellogg, who had previously identified himself as the manager of the Fleetwood Mall. "Good afternoon, this is Paul Kellogg. I'm calling to relay a small change of plans in regards to the speakers for the Christmas trees."

"Okay. What is going on?" asked Barrett.

"Our audio vender called me the other day and said he didn't have enough speakers to meet our needs. So, he put them on back order and expects them to arrive, late Thursday evening. Would it be alright if a delivery service provider meets your truck at the nursery before you leave for the Mall early Friday? I trust your people will put the speakers into the planters for me."

"I think we can do that. We plan to leave for the Mall around 7:00 a.m. Just make sure they arrive at the nursery in plenty of time, so we can put them inside the planters."

"That should not be a problem. Thanks for being so cooperative and helping me out."

"Glad to do it. Will you be at the Mall early Friday morning?"

"No, my hours are usually between 10:00 a.m. and 6:00 p.m., but we will probably meet in person sometime later. Merry Christmas, and Happy New Year, in case I don't see you before the Holidays are over," said Kellogg.

"Merry Christmas to you too, and thanks again for the business," he said, as he hung up the telephone. *What a nice fellow,* he thought to himself.

*   *   *

As discussed, Muqtadir checked in with Hastings on Wednesday morning, prior to Thanksgiving, to tell him how the plan was progressing. Hastings wanted to know specifically about Muqtadir's appraisal as to the combatants' readiness, whether or not the bus driver had been dealt with, if there were any problems, and if Khan had taken care of her responsibilities. Muqtadir assured him that things were moving along as planned and that he had just talked to the supervisors, who seemed optimistic. Prior to leaving the bus drivers home, he told Hastings that he had found the booking contract in the office filing cabinet and destroyed it. Khan had assured him, there was nothing left in her Grandville apartment to worry about. Hastings seemed please by Muqtadir's report and encouraged him to stay in touch, following the attack.

Overall, the mission had three defined goals. First, destroy the Cook Nuclear plant, killing and injuring as many people as possible. Second, scare the general population of the United States about their vulnerability in regards to al-Qaeda's reach. And third, secure and maintain their domestic informant as an agent for al-Qaeda. Hastings made an independent decision that there would be a fourth goal, to attack a local shopping mall. That portion of the operation had not been formally approved by al-Qaeda, but Hastings was sure their leaders would be very pleased if it too was successful. The good thing about it was that most of the labor involved in allowing the plan to proceed was being provided by innocent participants.

There was no reason to believe it would not injure or kill many unsuspecting shoppers, the day after Thanksgiving. Hastings knew the overall mission and its lofty goals were going to be difficult, but not unattainable to achieve.

Chapter 32

In the early morning hours of Thanksgiving, Thursday, November 27, 2003, the two al-Qaeda supervisors awoke their men, instructed them to dress, and assemble their equipment, in preparation for the attack. Before they got into the vans, and proceeded to their target, the supervisors led the men in their final prayers to Allah, asking for a successful mission. The Cook Nuclear Power Plant was about twenty minutes away. The temperatures were in the low thirties when they arrived at the target. The moon was waning and the surrounding grounds were dark, with the exception of the spot lights that illuminated the facility. It was quiet outside the compound, except for the sound of sparse traffic and the occasional whine of commercial trucks roaring up and down the expressway.

When they arrived at Cook, one of the two al-Qaeda supervisors instantly took command, pointed to four men, and said, "Kill the two guards at the main entrance, keep it quiet, and don't attract any undue attention." The men responded with a nod. Outside the fenced off perimeter, the terrorists jogged the short distance towards the guard house. When they arrived at the guard shack, two of the four men climbed over the fence. They signaled to each other that it was time to act, and then said, "God is great." They busted into the guard house, pointed their weapons at the unsuspecting guards, and shot and killed them. They had been instructed to shoot each guard, twice in the head. Their 9-mm hand guns were equipped with silencers, so there was no significant noise when they fired their rounds. Momentarily, they watched as blood quickly oozed out of the men's skulls and spread rapidly onto the ground. Once the guard house had been overtaken and secured, the other supervisor said, "Open the entrance gate, and drive the first van inside the facility." The men did as they were instructed, stopping the van briefly at the guard house. Meanwhile, the second van waited outside on Red Arrow Highway. Each van had previously been decaled with signage indicating they were from the Cook Nuclear facility. Two of the terrorists, from inside the second van, quickly emerged and set up orange safety cones, both in front and behind their vehicle, which partially blocked the entry way into the facility. They were dressed in military uniforms and appeared to be examining the main electrical lines on top of the poles, leading into Cook. "Stay here, observe, and secure the entrance at all cost," commanded the supervisor. The men signaled their acknowledgement with a wave and proceeded to do as they were instructed.

The supervisor pointed to the two attackers at the guard house and said, "You two, hide the bodies behind the shack and remain inside. Pretend to be security guards." The other two terrorists were instructed to sneak towards the second guard house on the roadway. The balance of the force followed behind the van, on foot. The second guard house was maintained by only one sentry and he was, thus far, not aware of the on-going attack. When the attackers arrived at the second guard house, the supervisor pointed to one of the two awaiting terrorists and said, "Kill the guard. He looks half-asleep; he'll never know what hit him." The terrorist nodded and quickly rushed through the unlocked door and shot the man twice between the eyes. "Hide his body behind the building," instructed the al-Qaeda supervisor. Then he directed the terrorist to position himself inside the shack, and pose as a sentry. That left fifteen combatants and the two supervisors to finish the job.

The surveillance done by Ashley Kahn indicated there was a roving force of about five armed Cook security guards that routinely exited the smaller building closest to the massive reactor building. The Cook guards had supposedly already made their rounds inside the perimeter, fifteen minutes prior to the attack. The heavily armed guards were not expected to reappear for another forty-five minutes. By this time, the remaining force had made its way to the second guard shack and were there awaiting instructions from their supervisors on when and how to proceed. The supervisor pointed to five more terrorists and said, "Take up offensive positions over there near the security building. Kill them all when they come out." That left twelve terrorists, including the supervisors, to attack the four towers. Once the towers were neutralized, the plan called for them to proceed inside the massive building, where the reactors were located.

Thus far, things seemed to be going as planned, both

supervisors thought. However, they did not realize that once the main gate was opened at night, the first guard house was supposed to reset the alarm within a minute and a half. When that was not done, a silent alarm was supposed to be activated in the security building. The half-asleep Cook guard that was supposed to be monitoring the television screens, said, "What the hell?" when he heard the alarm going off. He immediately began checking out the security screens from the cameras that were scattered around the facility. Once he sighted the vans, both inside and outside the facility, the security guard knew the complex had been compromised. The man had no idea how many intruders had entered the facility but assumed it was a substantial number. Within fifteen seconds, he activated a full alert to the local police departments, and to the other guards, inside the facility. Soon, the Homeland Security Department and the FBI would be notified, as well.

Unbeknownst to the terrorists, in about ten minutes, the entire facility would be swarming with various police enforcement personnel. In situations like this, the mandated security protocol at the Cook facility was to wait until reinforcements arrived, before the Cook security team would take action. Nevertheless, the guard towers were immediately notified about the intruders, and the two heavily armed guards located inside each tower, were instructed to be ready for an assault. The guard houses were also notified, via the deceased guard's handheld receiver. The terrorists, already stationed inside the guard houses, were confused as to whether or not they should try to notify their co-conspirators. By then, the main force was too far from the guard houses to be able to quickly warn them, in advance, the men thought.

Inside the reactor building, there was another guard station positioned next to the two rear access doors. Inside that station were four heavily armed guards, ready to defend the building and the reactors. The terrorists were out-manned and out-gunned without knowing it. Once the shooting started they would quickly realize the dire state of their situation. It had been a losing proposition from the very beginning. The attack had been poorly researched, improperly planned, and badly executed.

The unsuspecting terrorists waited for a brief time before trying to access the guard towers. They had hoped to be able to unlock the mechanisms that secured the tower doors, but they were unsuccessful. So, they used explosives to blow open the doors, which was about the time reinforcements began arriving at the facility. The two terrorists stationed outside on Red Arrow Highway, the three terrorists manning the guard houses, and the balance of the al-Qaeda forces were no match for the incoming law enforcement and Cook facility contingent.

As for the rest of the terrorists, they were sitting ducks for the guards in the towers. Once the fighting began, the guards fired repeatedly at the overwhelmed combatants, who opposed them. Bullets were flying inside the facility, and the gunfire was loud and unrelenting. The combatants fought hard, but were no match for the remaining guards and incoming police officers. Within ten minutes, the shooting was over, and twelve terrorists lay dead inside the grounds of the facility. Five more terrorists were seriously wounded, three had surrendered, and two were caught trying to get away. The two al-Qaeda supervisors had been killed early on, which meant they were unable to set off the suicide vests that the combatants were wearing.

About a half hour after the shooting had ceased, Homeland Security and the FBI arrived and took charge of the scene. The entry gate had already been secured, and the wounded and dead Cook guards, from the guard houses and inside the facility, were taken care of by the first responders. After the FBI and Homeland Security personnel arrived, they were immediately given possession of the captured prisoners that had been detained by the local authorities. The local authorities had also collected the wounded and deceased terrorists. A make shift morgue had been set up in a nearby gymnasium, and the deceased terrorists were taken there. The dead Cook guards were transferred to an area funeral home, for the time being. Several hours later, the Federal authorities began the task of interviewing those terrorists that did not require continued hospitalization. Those combatants who were not injured were immediately transported, in a heavily fortified police vehicle, to a Federal prison facility for questioning.

*   *   *

In New York City, al-Harbia sat glued to his television set, awaiting news of the Cook Nuclear Facility attack. Once the details of the unsuccessful attack were communicated by the media, he was frustrated and concerned. He knew that the leadership of al-Qaeda had expected a successful result, and this seemed like a total failure. He wondered, *will I be blamed and will they take steps to move against me.* He doubted they would react as drastically as he had just imagined. However, he knew that he needed to ensure that Hammoud, Khan, and Muqtadir would not be captured, imprisoned, and forced to talk.

Within several minutes, al-Harbia was on the telephone with the airlines scheduling a flight for the next day to Detroit. He felt the need to act very quickly before things got out of control.

Terrorists in the Heartland

Chapter 33

Back in Langdon, Michigan, Agents Johnson and Giordano were across the street from The General Store, in an abandoned building watching Hammoud. They had been there since Saturday night, November 22. To date, the surveillance operation had been unproductive. They had considered ending the operation and returning to Grand Rapids within the next several days.

It was early in the morning on Thursday, November 27, when Johnson received a call on his cell phone, informing him of the attack at Cook Power Plant. The attack had occurred about fifteen-minutes prior to the call. Immediately, he awoke Giordano and informed him about the unsuccessful assault conducted by unknown terrorists. The attack had been thwarted by local police agencies and the Cook security forces. Luckily, the reactors were intact and had not been damaged.

Johnson told Giordano, they had been directed by their superiors to obtain a search warrant for Hammoud's property in the hopes of finding contraband material. They immediately contacted a local magistrate, explained to him about the Cook attack, and secured a search warrant within an hour. They drove to Hammoud's residence. When they arrived they informed Hammoud that they had a search warrant for his residence, the Mosque, and the General Store. They told him it would be best for his family, if he cooperated with them immediately. Hammoud seemed nervous, but he willingly complied with their request. The agents did not disclose to him the reason for the search warrant or the attack at the Cook facility.

They began inspecting his residence. No contraband items were found there. Upon arriving at the store, the agents immediately began to inspect the property. Within an hour, they had uncovered the existence of two hidden storage spaces in the attic. Several weapons, three boxes of ammunition, and some communication equipment were found in one of the storage spaces. Both spaces had a distinct odor of gun powder still lingering inside.

Hammoud was taken into custody, handcuffed, and read his rights. He was incarcerated at the local Marshall's office in Langdon. Giordano and Johnson began their criminal interrogation of him concerning his involvement and affiliation with terrorists groups. Giordano began, "Mr. Hammoud, you realize that you are in serious trouble, don't you?"

Hammoud was silent. He sat there and listened as agent Johnson commented to him, "The United States government will be putting you away for many years, as a terrorist co-conspirator. Your life and your family's lives will be ruined. If you cooperate with us now, and tell us what you know, we are authorized to offer you a deal," he said.

"What kind of deal?" asked Hammoud.

"A deal that would allow you and your family to stay in the United States and avoid being deported on terrorist charges," said Giordano. "However, you would still have to go away for several years, but your family would be provided for and protected from retaliation. It's up to you."

"How many years would I have to serve in jail?" asked Hammoud.

"That depends on how well you cooperate with us," said Giordano. "If you tell us everything you know about this operation, and not lie about it, the government will be more apt to offer leniency." He told Hammoud what he imagined the man would like to hear. In actuality, he believed the United States government would want to lock him up and throw away the keys, for as long as possible. Giordano also wondered if Hammoud's family would ultimately be deported back to Iraq, in the end.

"What assurances do I have that you are going to do what you say, if I talk?" asked Hammoud.

"If you cooperate, we will work with the United States Attorney General's office to make sure you get the minimum sentence. But, you need to tell us now before the bureaucrats get involved in this matter," said Johnson.

"I'd like to have that in writing before I tell you anything," said Hammoud.

"We should be able to have that for you in a few hours," Johnson assured him.

The following morning, Giordano returned to Hammoud's jail cell with a large manila envelope in his hand. "This deal has been approved by the Attorney General of the United States of American. Take a look at it, and let me know what you want to do," he said. "I'll be awaiting your response."

After a half an hour, Hammoud summoned Giordano back to his jail cell. "Is that the best deal I am going to get?" he asked.

"Yes, it is," said Giordano, bluntly.

"I guess I don't have much of a choice then," he said.

"You will be making the best deal for you and your family," said Giordano. "Before we get started, I'm going to set up a recorder and camera to document your testimony."

"That's fine. What do you want to know?" asked Hammoud.

Giordano ignored Hammoud as he took a few minutes to set up. After he finished, he began questioning Hammoud.

"For this operation, who was your supervisor/al-Qaeda contact?" asked Giordano.

"His name is Abdul Muqtadir. He resides and operates an independent sales business in Dearborn, Michigan."

"Do you know his address in Dearborn?"

"No, I do not, but I have his phone number," claimed Hammoud.

"How long have you known him?"

"About fifteen years. He helped me financially after I arrived in Dearborn, in the late 1980's. My business there had failed and he was the one who helped me get back on my feet. Several other friends from the Mosque I attended in Dearborn helped me too, but not as significantly as Muqtadir did."

"Were your other friends at the Mosque associated with al-Qaeda at the time?"

"No, I don't think so. As far as I know, only Abdul was involved with al-Qaeda," said Hammoud.

"Who was in charge of this operation?

"I made the arrangement with al-Qaeda through Abdul. He asked me to help him set up a cell to be used to store weapons and materials in Langdon, needed for future al-Qaeda operations."

"When did you modify the attic to accommodate the materials, and when were the weapons and contraband delivered to The General Store?"

"Originally, I made the deal in 2000, but Muqtadir did not start pressing me to create a cell, until late 2002. The modifications to the attic were completed this year, with the help of my men. The first and only shipment I ever received was delivered a few months ago, and picked up last weekend. Muqtadir arranged for his men to do the work.

"Do you know any of their names?"

"No, I do not. I was never introduced."

"Where did those materials come from?" inquired Giordano.

"I believe Muqtadir procured them and was responsible for overseeing their delivery to me. Prior to the operation, he arranged to have them picked up. I assume he was the one in charge."

"What operation are you talking about?" inquired Giordano. *I wonder if Hammoud knew about the attack at the Cook Nuclear facility, earlier in the day. It seems as if maybe he didn't,* imagined Giordano.

"Muqtadir alluded to needing the weapons and contraband for an on-going operation, which I assumed was about to occur."

"I can tell you that an al-Qaeda operation occurred early this morning. Fortunately, it was not successful. What do you know about that operation?"

"I know absolutely nothing about it. I assume the weapons and materials that they used had been the same ones they stored in my attic."

"Are you asking me to believe you knew nothing about this current operation?" stated Giordano.

"Yes. I'm telling you I knew nothing about it. I have no idea where or what the operation consisted of. Don't you know? That is how al-Qaeda operates. They don't tell many others, outside of high rank, the details of their plans. At least that is what I have been told."

"Who else in Langdon was aware of the operation or involved with al-Qaeda?" asked Giordano.

"I talked three other men into helping me modify the attic space, but they know less than I do. They were never associated with al-Qaeda, like I was," said Hammoud.

"Who are they?"

"They are long-time friends of mine, from Dearborn. Please do not involve them, because they were just trying to help me out. They did not know this involved al-Qaeda," claimed Hammoud.

Giordano sensed Hammoud was lying to protect them and he asked for their names. Hammoud reluctantly complied with his request. *I'll deal with them later*, thought Giordano. Hammoud continued with his testimony before telling Giordano and Johnson that Muqtadir was a dangerous man, with a sinister reputation, and capable of doing anything, including murder.

During the interview, Giordano told Hammoud that he was going to take a break from the process and get something to drink. He left the room and quickly provided the information Hammoud had given him, concerning Muqtadir, to the FBI field office in Detroit. Giordano suggested that the Bureau pick up Muqtadir immediately for questioning. Several hours later, the Detroit office communicated back to Giordano that they had been unable to locate Muqtadir, his home, his business, or find out who had set up his phone service. The name on the account was someone other than Abdul Muqtadir, and when they researched it, the name was fictitious too. They also found out that the phone number had been cancelled, several days prior to the attack. They assured Giordano that they would immediately notify him if they made any progress in their search for Muqtadir.

Chapter 34

At 6:30 a.m., November 28, a gray delivery van approached the Pine Valley Tree Farm and pulled into a parking space in front of the building. The logo on both sides of the van read, "Douglas Inter-State Delivery." Before departing the van, the driver grabbed a clipboard from inside and headed towards the office door. As he passed by his vehicle, he noticed there was still frost on the fenders, side panels, and top. The temperature was in the low-thirties, and the bright Friday morning sun had just begun to melt the fine glaze of ice off the van. One of the tree farm laborers greeted him at the counter, signed his paperwork, and instructed him to bring the cargo to the rear of the building. The delivery man complied.

Five minutes later, the driver unloaded six boxes marked Harmon Kardon professional acoustical speakers onto the truck dock. Each box marked fragile, contained a speaker, and measured over one foot cubed. The farm employee lifted them onto the trailer, with the six Christmas trees that were already secured for transport. Each tree, as requested, was planted in a large wooden barrel container.

"Thanks for your help," said the driver to the farm employee.

A few minutes later, James Barrett, the tree farm owner, emerged from the building. He handed a diagram of the Mall to his employee and said, "Make sure the trees are positioned in the Mall according to the instructions on this drawing. And please, ensure that each speaker is placed in front of the tree trunks in the planters, after being set into place."

"Will do Boss," said the employee. Several minutes later, the heavy-duty truck and trailer, containing the six trees with speakers, was on its way towards The Fleetwood Mall.

The Fleetwood Mall is the oldest, most popular, and busiest shopping complex in Kalamazoo, Michigan. It features four major department stores that anchor each corner of the rectangular shaped Mall. In addition, there are approximately thirty smaller specialty chain stores, located on each level. The lower level shops of the two-story Mall reside underground. There are three escalators that move retail patrons from the street level shops on the upper level, down to the lower level shopping area. On the lower level, a large and very popular ten-store food court occupies the central section. The upper level of the Mall caters both to youth and adult patrons. The stores on the lower level cater primarily to young children and teens.

The Mall is about a half-hour drive from the tree farm. When the truck and trailer arrived at the Mall parking lot, the driver quickly located the north-side delivery area and backed the trailer up to the delivery dock. He and another tree farm employee got out of the truck and found a part-time Mall employee, working inside the building. The driver showed the Mall employee the tree placement diagram they had received from James Barrett, the tree farm owner. The employee claimed he was unaware of the delivery but decided that the lack of communication was sometimes to be expected during the holidays. *As big as these speakers are, they must be really expensive,* thought the farm employee, as he helped to lift them off the trailer and onto the dock. *Considering the tree, planters, and speaker, these things weigh a ton,* he thought. Within thirty-minutes, the two tree farm employees had positioned the Christmas trees, inside the Mall. Several minutes later, they departed the Mall parking lot.

The Mall employee had been told, by the tree farm laborers, that the Mall manager had arranged for the delivery of the trees, a few weeks before. So, after the delivery and tree placement had been completed, the employee went to the manager's office to drop off the paperwork. The secretary was unaware of the tree purchase as well, but she told the part-time employee, the Mall manager would be in sometime after noon. The secretary assumed the purchase of the trees was to enhance the spirit of the Christmas Season for all the Mall employees and patrons. She assured the young man that she would give the Mall manager the message that the trees had been placed and delivered as per his instructions. Frankly, the manager's secretary was curious about the timing of the purchase for the additional Christmas trees, but she knew it was not wise to question the manager's instructions. Within several hours, the manager would return and she would bring up the subject.

All the stores were expecting big crowds after Thanksgiving. What they were not expecting, however, was what ensued several hours after the Mall opened that Friday morning. The six trees had been placed in such a manner that each major department store had a Christmas tree placed near the interior doorways inside the Mall, on the lower level of the Mall complex. The other two were placed in the center of the Mall, on each side of the food court.

At precisely 8:00 a.m., the Mall opened for business. People displayed smiles and feelings of Holiday cheer as they proceeded to their favorite stores. All were in the holiday mood and were there shopping for wonderful gifts for their family and friends. Around 11:50 a.m., when the Mall was overflowing with people, six loud explosions were heard inside the Mall complex, originating from the lower level. When the dust settled, hundreds of people lay either wounded or dead amongst the broken glass and rubble. Store windows were blown out, sprinkler systems were spurting water everywhere, and merchandise was strewn about. Panic ensued amongst those who were in the Mall at the time of the explosions. Moans and screams could be heard from those that were wounded. Cries were heard from the loved ones who survived and were cradling their dead in their arms. Children were weeping at the sight of their injured or dead parents, siblings, and friends, who lay helplessly on the ground. Briefly after the explosions there was a weird sense of quietness that prevailed amongst the death and destruction. Thirty seconds later, the survivors began to help the wounded and comfort the dying. Most able survivors began calling 911 on their cell phones. Within fifteen minutes, the building was surrounded by police and fire department vehicles. Almost immediately, ambulances arrived outside the Mall and the EMT's began to transport the wounded to area hospitals for treatment. Much of the damage from the bombs had been caused as a result of the bomb-maker using solid metal objects, such as, nails, screws, razor blades, and bolts, inside the speaker compartments.

Immediately following the explosions, the local and Michigan State Police, along with Homeland Security and the FBI, were notified. An investigative team from the Grand Rapids FBI office was immediately dispatched to the Mall in Kalamazoo. However, Giordano and Johnson were not included in this investigation. They were already busy investigating the Cook facility attack. Once he learned about the explosions at the Mall, Giordano assumed that the two incidents were related and he communicated his suspicions to Tom Murrell, his superior in Grand Rapids. He reasoned that Abdul Muqtadir was involved in planning both the Fleetwood Mall attack as well as the Cook attack, but he could not prove it. Giordano was hopeful the FBI in Dearborn would be able to find and hold Muqtadir for questioning, concerning both attacks. However, he was certain that Muqtadir was already in hiding from the authorities, for obvious reasons. *He wondered if Hammoud had any knowledge of the Fleetwood Mall attack. It seemed apparent that the supplies needed to make six bombs had not come from*

Hammoud's attic space, according to Hammoud's sworn testimony. According to Hammoud, he stated he did not receive any bulk gun powder or any screws or nails that could have been used in making bombs. Giordano doubted that Muqtadir was the bomb-maker in addition to being the planner? But, he knew they needed to quickly find Muqtadir before he completely disappeared into thin air.

Chapter 35

After learning about the absolute failure at the Cook Nuclear facility, through news coverage on all the major television channels, al-Harbia boarded a flight the following day to Detroit, Michigan. He had already decided that some of the major players, who had participated in the attack, might require help to ensure their safety and obscurity. The television broadcasts were full of news coverage concerning both the Cook and Fleetwood Mall attacks. He also knew that the majority of the combatants had been killed or injured but that there were some that had been captured. Al-Harbia was not too concerned about what information the authorities might have gleaned from the combatants alone. However, he was worried about Hammoud, Khan, and Muqtadir, in particular. Under the right circumstances, his existence and obscurity might be in jeopardy too. If all of them were captured and interrogated, the authorities might be able to connect all the dots, with help from the combatants' testimony, as well.

Unfortunately, he had learned of the arrest of several

people connected with the incident, who lived in Langdon, Michigan. The authorities were not releasing any names, but al-Harbia assumed they had already arrested Hammoud and his co-conspirators, and they were presently being questioned. Since Muqtadir had already assured al-Harbia that the bus driver had been eliminated, he was somewhat relieved. *One less person to worry about,* he thought. Nevertheless, he knew the al-Qaeda contacts in Canada were involved, but Canada was not his problem or concern.

Upon his arrival in Detroit, he was sure Muqtadir was hiding somewhere by now. Previously in the day, he had been able to contact Muqtadir and arrange for an accident to occur at the residence of Ashley Khan. *Hopefully, the accident will get rid of her permanently,* he thought. Al-Harbia assumed that would not be a problem for Muqtadir, who was skilled at those types of things. He had instructed him to be sure it looked like an accident. Muqtadir assured him it would not be a problem. The pair agreed to meet later that evening to discuss Muqtadir's future, following the Cook attack. They settled on meeting at a small neighborhood Italian restaurant, in North Detroit. Al-Harbia assured Muqtadir that he still had a bright future with al-Qaeda, although, he would need to be relocated. The meeting was scheduled for 9:00 p.m. Al-Harbia had given him assurances that al-Qaeda was going to help him with money, new identification papers, travel vouchers, and relocation to another city. As a condition for that help, Muqtadir had to agree to kill Khan, prior to his departure, as part of his final responsibilities. Muqtadir was somewhat concerned about al-Harbia's visit, but felt comforted by al-Harbia's calming nature and apparent genuine concern for his welfare that he perceived in their phone conversation.

*   *   *

When Muqtadir arrived at Ernesto's Italian restaurant, he parked in an adjacent lot, next to restaurant. The dead-end street, where the restaurant was located, seemed quiet with the exception of an occasional vehicle or two, passing by the location. It was just before 9:00 p.m. and he got out of his car and approached the front door to the restaurant. Muqtadir briefly looked in the front window and saw several couples and two individuals eating inside. An overly plump waitress appeared, carrying a plate of antipasto to the single man, sitting in the back booth. He could not see the man's face, but it did not matter. He had never met al-Harbia before, but the man did not appear to look mid-eastern. Muqtadir went inside and took a seat at the vacant booth, next the front door. The waitress walked over to his table and inquired, "What can I get you to drink?"

"A coke with lots of ice, please," he responded.

"Sure thing," she said. "Take a look at our menu, and I'll be back to take your order."

"Thanks," said Muqtadir politely. A few minutes later, a dark complected, mid-eastern man came into the restaurant and approached his table. The man looked him over briefly and asked, "Are you Abdul?"

"Yes. Are you Hastings?"

"Yes. It's nice to finally meet," he said. "Have you eaten?" he asked, as he sat down, across from the man.

"No, I'm not really hungry, but I just ordered a coke."

"Well, the sooner we can take care of business, the sooner I can be back to New York City," said al-Harbia.

"Have you worked out all the details for my relocation?" Muqtadir asked.

"Yes, I have taken care of everything," he said. "We can talk here for a while, drink a coke, and then get you on your way to a new life and location. How does that sound?"

"It sounds wonderful!"

"Thankfully, Allah has a way of always providing what we need," said al-Harbia. "Did you meet with Ms. Khan?"

"Yes, I discovered there was a problem with her out-dated water heater in the apartment. It had, unbeknownst to her, developed a serious gas leak. When she got home today around 5:30 p.m. and turned on the light switch, the static electricity ignited the excess natural gas in her apartment. There was a terrible explosion, and she undoubtedly succumbed to the smoke and flames."

"Is she dead?"

"Yes," commented Muqtadir.

"How do you know that?"

"Her apartment building was completely destroyed in the blaze. I watched as the coroner hauled her body away," said Muqtadir. "The body bag was visible inside the coroner's van. No one else was treated on the scene or taken away in an ambulance."

"Good news, but what a shame. I had high hopes for her success," claimed al-Harbia. He looked appreciably at Muqtadir and said, "Thank you Abdul. I know I can always count on you, my friend." Muqtadir perceived that al-Harbia sounded relieved. "Are you ready to go?" he asked.

"Sure, I'm ready," said Muqtadir. When they got outside, al-Harbia accompanied Muqtadir to his car and handed him a small envelope.

"Inside this envelope is a key for a storage locker at the main bus terminal, in downtown Detroit," said al-Harbia. In the locker, you will find instructions to help you relocate, my new phone number, a sizeable amount of cash, new identification papers, travel vouchers, a new cell phone, and plans for your relocation to Cleveland, Ohio. Do you have any questions?"

"No, I don't think so. Thank you for all your help, my brother," he said, as he briefly embraced the man.

"Safe travels and good luck. I'll be in touch," said al-Harbia.

Al-Harbia watched as Muqtadir put the envelope into his coat pocket and turned to get into his vehicle. A few seconds later, he turned back to acknowledge Hastings again. But, what he saw startled him. Hastings was pointing a small caliber revolver equipped with a silencer at his head.

"What are you doing?" Muqtadir exclaimed frantically.

"Goodbye, my brother," said al-Harbia, as he pulled the trigger and shot Muqtadir several times in the frontal part of his head. Muqtadir's body immediately fell to the ground. After retrieving his wallet, car keys, and the envelope from his pockets, al-Harbia dragged Muqtadir to the rear of his vehicle and lifted it into the trunk. He closed the trunk, and then looked around to see if there were any witnesses to deal with. Seeing none, he slowly turned and got into Muqtadir's vehicle and drove away.

A half hour later, he stopped the car outside a large auto salvage yard and waited for a signal to drive inside. Within a few minutes, two dark skinned men approached his car, opened the gate, and waved him inside the yard. Al-Harbia got out of the car and briefly talked to the men. He retrieved five hundred dollars from his wallet and handed it to one of the men. The other man got into the vehicle, and al-Harbia watched as he drove the car around to the front of a large car crushing machine and got out. The man climbed onto the machine and turned it on. Soon, a large crane attached to the machine, swung around, and picked up the vehicle with an electro- magnetic circular device. The vehicle was picked up and lowered onto a large conveyor track on the machine. Five minutes later, a crushed steel cube about three feet square, emerged from the device. Al-Harbia thanked the man, walked over to his rental vehicle, and drove away.

An hour later, he pulled into the Detroit International Airport and parked the rental car in the National rental return parking lot. He paid the attendant, and departed via a transit bus that took him back to the American Airlines terminal. As he sat at the departure gate, he wondered. *Will the al-Qaeda leaders be happy with my decisions? He hoped the excellent results at Fleetwood Mall would be enough to appease his superiors, as they thought about the failed attack at Cook.*

Terrorists in the Heartland

Chapter 36

Before the news of the blasts at Fleetwood Mall had been made public, the FBI, ATF, Homeland Security, and other government officials had already been notified. The Mall was temporarily closed to store owners and patrons, as the investigation continued. There was an emergency action plan put into place. Over the next several days, investigators from those departments in Washington, D.C., began to swarm the Fleetwood Mall and around the Cook Nuclear facility. Their purpose at Cook was to supplement the on-going investigation by agent Frank Giordano. Giordano had been appointed the lead agent, by Tom Murrell, the Grand Rapids FBI supervising agent in charge. Neal Johnson was acting as Giordano's official assistant, on the case. The Fleetwood Mall attack was being handled by other officials from the FBI, ATF, and the local and state-wide police agencies, in Michigan.

Three days into the post-investigation of the attack at Cook, Giordano and his staff had compiled a considerable amount of information. After interrogating Hammoud, his men, and the combatants, they were able to locate the warehouse where the operation had been staged from. Through that information, they had talked to the real estate agent, Kay Sanders, who had set up the rental agreement for Axis Equipment Corporation. Sanders verified she had been working with a Marsha Showalter, the CEO's secretary, in Battle Creek, Michigan. After contacting the CEO of Axis, his secretary, and Kay Sanders, the agents deduced the operation had been a hoax. The real Marsha Showalter had no idea these things had been taking place. Unbeknownst to Showalter, her name had been used by Khan. Sanders had been told the rental facility was to temporarily store Axis' increased production needs.

The female operative, who had set up the phony lease, was not able to be identified. Apparently, her conversations with the real estate agent were traced back to a pay phone in the downtown Grand Rapids area. She had never met in person with anyone. All the arrangements were handled via the telephone, thus she could not be identified.

While being interrogated, one of the combatants remembered the name of the bus company that had been used to transfer them from Canada to the United States border. The Canadian authorities had been allowed to interview the combatants, and the police were pursuing leads that they had gleaned, during their interrogation. It was determined that once in the United States, the combatants had been driven across the Mackinac Bridge, by a locally owned United States bus company.

Ultimately, it was discovered the combatant team had been selected and trained by a high ranking Al-Qaeda official in Afghanistan. They were flown to Toronto,

Canada, through Pakistan and France. First, a Canadian bus company and then a United States bus company had been used to transport them to Stevensville, Michigan. The location of the small American bus company that transported them was found in the Mackinaw City area. Several days later, the body of the bus driver/owner operator was located, buried in a freshly dug grave, about a half mile behind his place of business.

As for the acquisition of the weapons and equipment, most all of the items, with the exception of the weaponry, could have been acquired almost anywhere. He assumed the weapons, ammunition, and explosives had been purchased in the black market.

It was verified Muqtadir met the combatants at the United States border, helped transport them to the warehouse, arranged for the rental of the warehouse, acquired the weapons and equipment, and directed the entire operation for al-Qaeda.

The authorities had been able to acquire a detailed drawing of Muqtadir's face and description, through the cooperation and testimony of the two combatants that were talking. The others were scared and afraid of repercussions against their families if they provided information to the authorities, about al-Qaeda. Giordano was hopeful the drawing would eventually lead to the capture of Muqtadir.

Unfortunately, the investigators had been unable to identify who he really was from the drawing. It was assumed that he had been using a false name. When they showed his drawing to the Imam and members of the Dearborn Mosque, where he had reportedly attended, no one seemed to recognize him. They were either covering up for him, shielding his real identity, or they were being truthful. The authorities were told that it was common for former or past members to have attended several Mosques, according to their schedules. Giordano was not surprised; he had anticipated little or no help from the Dearborn Muslim community, anyway.

Without the ability to locate and interrogate Muqtadir, Giordano realized the investigation had come to a screeching halt. He thought about all the leads that had been developed by his investigatory team. Yet, they still had been unable to identify or arrest any of the major players. Unfortunately, Hammoud, his men, and the combatants were the only people in custody and awaiting trials. The combatants' two supervisors had been killed during the attack, so they were not going to be questioned.

As for the investigation into the Fleetwood Mall terrorist attack, there were very few helpful leads that would develop. The Christmas tree purchase had been made over the telephone by someone claiming to be Mr. Paul Kellogg, the Fleetwood Mall manager. His identity was unable to be determined by the available information. Payment for the trees, barrels, and delivery cost was received by money order prior to delivery. The individual who sold the money order could not remember the transaction, and there was no video tape to review. The call from the person claiming to be Mr. Kellogg to Mr. Barrett, the tree farm owner, was traced to a pay phone in the Grand Rapids downtown area.

The Harmon Kardon speakers were probably purchased

at a large chain or retail establishment outside of Grand Rapids. However, they had been unable to verify the distributor, for the reason that the serial numbers were destroyed in the blasts and the boxes the speakers were shipped in had already been destroyed, at the tree farm.

Apparently, the bomb maker had filled the speaker containers with nails, screws, razor blades, and bolts, commonly available through any chain hardware or name brand retailer. Their origin was unable to be determined.

The delivery arrangements for the speakers that had been dropped off at the Douglas Inter-State Delivery company had been made by John Delman, who signed the paperwork. At the time, the clerk questioned why a pastor would be arranging for the speakers to be delivered to the Pine Valley Tree Farm. It just seemed odd to her, and the man had paid the fee in cash. The whole transaction seemed weird, she remembered thinking. The clerk recalled Delman was a good-looking African American. She remembered him wearing a white collar and a black clergy shirt and being pleasant and polite. Unfortunately, she could remember nothing else. The delivery service office had been extremely busy that day and she almost had forgotten about it, by the time she went home.

The tree farm laborer, who had placed the speakers into the Christmas tree barrels, loaded them on the truck, and hauled them into the Mall, could only recall the speakers being extremely heavy. He apologized to the investigator over and over because of the extreme damage those bombs had done to the community. Eventually, he too was cleared of any responsibility in the attack.

The bomb detonators were simple timing devices used for a variety of things not necessarily associated with making bombs. They were available at every Radio Shack or chain electronic equipment store, nationwide.

Early on, Giordano had provided the name of Abdul Muqtadir, as a possible suspect behind the bombings at the Fleetwood Mall. Unfortunately, there was nothing that tied him to the blasts. To date, no terrorist organization had taken credit for the attack. The lead investigator for the Fleetwood incident was not ruling out the possibility of some nut case, who previously may have been affiliated with the Mall, as the culprit. The bombing may have occurred as the result of a grudge.

Overall, the authorities had compiled a plethora of data on both attacks, and they did not seem to be any closer to solving either case. The investigations continued, but over time, the authorities seemed perplexed as to whether or not they were ever going to arrest or prosecute any of the major players, including Muqtadir, who were undoubtedly lurking behind in the shadows.

Chapter 37

Several weeks after the attacks, Mohammed al-Harbia, sent a lengthy report to his al-Qaeda superiors back in Afghanistan. In the report, he blamed Abdul Muqtadir, for the failure to execute the Cook Nuclear plan properly, for the incomplete intelligence provided to the planners, and for his failure to develop the terrorist's cells, in the United States, in a timely manner.

Al-Harbia indicated that it was he who was responsible for the development and implementation of the successful attack at the Fleetwood Mall. He stated that one of their new recruits had successfully over-seen the operation, with his help and guidance. He was sure the Al-Qaeda leadership would be happy he had taken the initiative to carry out, what came to be, a very successful, injurious, and lethal event at the Mall.

Al-Harbia also claimed responsibility for getting rid of Muqtadir, Ashley Khan, and the bus operator, who they had used to transport the combatant team from Canada to Stevensville, Michigan. Al-Harbia also indicated Najeeb Hammoud had been taken into custody, and the report stated that he assumed Najeeb was cooperating with the authorities.

*　　*　　*

That same week after the attacks, Neal Johnson received a phone call from his girlfriend, LaToya Smith, late in the evening. When he answered the call, LaToya said, "Hey stranger. I've been in town for more than several days. Why haven't you called me back?"

"I'm really sorry, I've been meaning to. My boss has had me so busy at work, all I want to do is come home from work and sleep," said Johnson. "Please forgive me."

"Well, I didn't know you were that busy. I guess I'll forgive you," she said, sounding half-way reluctant. "We need to talk about something important."

"Before we have that discussion, I have some bad news to tell you about. My Mother died several weeks ago in Dearborn, due to an unexpected accident that occurred at her home."

"Oh my God, Neal," said LaToya, dramatically as she tried to act surprised and shocked. "How did it happen, and why didn't you tell me?"

"There was an old water heater in her apartment, and it had apparently become an increasing problem, overtime. The fumes from the leak finally ignited and a terrible explosion occurred. Pausing briefly, he said, "There were no survivors."

Johnson went on to say, "I figured you had enough problems and your own concerns to deal with. It was a very difficult situation for me to deal with, and frankly, I wanted to wait to tell you in person. I'm sorry, I made a mistake."

"I'm so sorry for your loss," LaToya said, sounding very sympathetic.

"My Mother was a Muslim and to her, death was simply a part of life. But, it's not a part of life for me, and I'm really going to miss her. In addition, my increased workload, along with handling my Mother's estate, has been almost unbearable to me. She was Yemeni, and her desire was to be buried in her former homeland, with her relatives. It has been quite a process, making those arrangements."

"I had no idea," she said.

"Look, I know I haven't paid enough attention to you lately," said Johnson.

"It's not about that honey," she said. "I got it. You are really busy at work and with these personal matters too. That is not the problem."

"What is it then?" asked Johnson.

"I've been offered the job of a lifetime in Japan working for a large United States firm, as their head flight stewardess."

"That sounds great," said Johnson.

"They have promised to double my current salary," she said. "The problem is my flight crew would be home-based in Japan, and not the United States."

"I see," said Johnson, sounding somewhat forlorn and confused. "How often would I be able to see you then?"

"Not very much, I'm afraid. That is why I wanted to talk to you. Is there any reason why I shouldn't consider taking this opportunity?" LaToya asked, sounding like she was probing for something.

After pausing for a half minute, Neal responded, "I don't know, but I'm not sure either one of us is ready for a long-term commitment, if that's what you are hinting at. Maybe you should take the job, he said, sounding frustrated. It sounds like a good opportunity for you. What do you think?"

"Well ... I guess I'm not quite ready to be married yet, either. However, I had thought I meant more to you than that," she said, sounding puzzled and confused.

"Look LaToya, you mean a great deal to me, but I'm not ready to settle down and start a family. After all, we've only known each other for a couple of months."

"Well, does this mean you want to end our relationship?" asked LaToya, soundly like she was on the verge of being upset.

"No. Not exactly, but let's just give ourselves some time and see how we feel in six months."

"Six months!" she blurted out. "That's not what I expected to hear from you," she said. "If that's how you really feel let's just end it now," she said reluctantly. I'm sorry this development is coming at such a terrible time for you emotionally."

"I'm sorry too," he said. "But, I'm still willing to see how things are between us in six months. Are you?"

"I guess we can see," she said, sounding slightly detached. "Goodbye Neil," she said, as she slowly hung up the receiver. After several seconds, she shed some tears and then wiped her eyes. *It probably ended up for the best, considering the circumstances*, she thought.

*   *   *

Giordano received a call from his former division chief in Washington, D.C., after he had turned over the Cook investigation to another agent. After his former Chief greeted Giordano with a minimal amount of small talk, he said. "Frank, I have some good news I'd like to discuss with you. Due to your excellent work on the Cook case, your organizational skills, and the arrest/conviction rate of the men involved, you are going back to FBI headquarters. Not only for your work on the Cook case, but also because it appears you were unjustly accused and punished for something you did not do, in regards to the Moussaoui incident. In addition, the Bureau is rewarding you for your assistance on the Johnson probe. So, effective immediately, it is my pleasure to tell you, you are going to be given a promotion, and be reassigned. Is that alright with you?"

"It sure is," said Frank. "Thanks for helping me out." To Frank, the words promotion and reassignment could not have come soon enough, nor could those words have been any sweeter. He was tired of Grand Rapids, and was pleased with the idea of a new assignment.

Frank did wonder, however, what might be in store for Neal Johnson. As far as he knew, Johnson was still under investigation. Nevertheless, Giordano had never bought into the notion that Neal was a spy, working for al-Qaeda or others. A month later, he was not surprised to learn that Johnson had been reassigned to the Detroit FBI Field Office. He wondered if that action was being taken to limit his access to the vast amount of information available in Washington, D.C. Regardless, Giordano believed that Johnson's skills, talents, and experience could be more effectively utilized in the heavily populated Muslim community of Detroit, Michigan.

Chapter 38

Three months after the attacks, al-Harbia flew back to Dearborn, Michigan, to meet with the operative that had coordinated the attack at Fleetwood Mall. They had agreed to meet on Sunday, in the late afternoon, at the Henry Ford Museum/Greenfield Village complex. The complex is located in Dearborn, and the museum is the largest indoor/outdoor history museum in the United States.

The historic National Landmark Museum has collections containing the presidential limousine of John F. Kennedy, Abraham Lincoln's chair from the Ford Theatre, Thomas Edison's laboratory, the Wright Brothers' bicycle shop, the Rosa Parks bus, and many more historical exhibits. Al-Harbia instructed his operative to meet him precisely at 4:00 p.m., on the park bench overlooking the Kennedy limousine that carried Kennedy during the assassination.

Al-Harbia arrived at the museum around 3:00 p.m. Arriving an hour early allowed him time to casually stroll by some of the more popular exhibits. Despite his limited tour of the complex, he found it very interesting and impressive. At 3:55 p.m. he sat down on the park bench overlooking the limousine, and waited for his operative to arrive.

At exactly 4:00 p.m., a tall, fairly handsome, African American gentleman appeared and sat down on the park bench next to him. Initially, neither man looked at each other, spoke, or acknowledged each other's presence. Finally, al-Harbia broke the silence and said, "I still can't believe how incredible it must have been to witness the assassination of one of our greatest Presidents. Something one would never be able to forget."

"I agree," said, the well-dressed black man. "He was so loved by most in the black community and by the entire nation."

"At least, that's what most people thought at the time," said al-Harbia, with a tone of disbelief in his voice. "Can you imagine what Lee Harvey Oswald thought as he gripped the sniper rifle that day? It must have been exhilarating to pull that trigger. Unfortunately, I am a terrible shot," al-Harbia admitted.

"You're probably doing what suits you best and fits your talents," said the unidentified man.

Lowering his voice, al-Harbia responded, "It's nice to finally meet you in person. My associates call me Hastings, and I know who you are."

"Nice to meet you too," said the stranger.

A half minute later, Al-Harbia reached into his pocket and retrieved an over-stuffed white envelope, filled with hundred dollar bills. He placed the envelope on the park bench between himself and the operative. "I deeply appreciate your remarkable oversight on the Fleetwood project, and so do my associates," he said, quietly. Just consider this a little bonus on top of your regular monthly payment.

"Thank you," said the man, as he nonchalantly picked up the envelope and casually slide it into the inside pocket of his suit jacket.

"As I said, my associates are very pleased with you and your expressed commitment to them," al-Harbia stated. "They also wanted me to pass on their condolences concerning the tragic loss of your Mother."

"I appreciate that very much, and I am slowly beginning to accept the loss, as time goes along."

"My personal condolences to you, as well," said al-Harbia. "With Allah's help, things will get better, my brother," he said. "You will see."

"Thank you, I am praying for Allah's blessings and intercession," said the operative.

"My associates asked me to convey that they are looking forward to a long, productive, and prosperous relationship going forward," said al-Harbia.

"Thank you Mr. Hastings," said the operative. "In the future, I hope to keep you informed, as best I can, about the governments activities concerning al-Qaeda."

"I look forward to continuing our important work together and I'll be in touch," said al-Harbia. Then, he abruptly arose, without acknowledging the man, and walked toward the main entrance of the museum. Several minutes later, the operative got up, looked around, and walked toward another exit, on the opposite side of the building.

Chapter 39

The operative departed the museum amongst a crowd of people and walked toward his vehicle, which was parked near the back of the lot. He was pleased hearing that al-Qaeda was glad to have him working for them. Plus, their monthly payments were attractive and more than adequate.

As he approached his vehicle, he noticed a Caucasian middle-aged man, who was sitting in a wheelchair. He appeared to be having trouble opening up the rear cargo door of his gray SUV. As he turned to walk towards the man's SUV, the man gestured to him and said, "Excuse me sir. I think my cargo door is jammed. Could you help me, please?"

"Sure, I'll try," said the operative, politely. "Glad to do it." When he attempted to open the door, it popped right up. "I guess I have the right touch," he said.

To his surprise, the man in the wheelchair, arose, pointed a gun at him, and said, "Neil Johnson, I'm agent Miller, with the FBI and you are under arrest for the

Fleetwood Mall bombing in Kalamazoo, Michigan. Put up your hands where I can see them, turn around, lean forward, and put your hands on the truck."

"There must be some mistake," said Johnson, as Miller frisked him, removed his service revolver, and placed him in handcuffs. "I'm with the FBI too," Johnson said.

"Unfortunately, I know you are," said Miller, as he Mirandized him. Within seconds, four other agents in dark suits quickly appeared and placed him into the middle seat of the SUV. Two of the men got in and sat on either side of him, in the second row. Agent Miller climbed into the vehicle and sat in the front passenger seat. Another agent quickly got into the driver's seat and drove away.

After several minutes Miller turned around and looked at Johnson and said, "No, there is no mistake, Mr. Johnson. Or, should I call you Pastor Delman or how about Paul Kellogg?" Johnson remained quiet, but had a startled and fearful look on his face. "We are going to take you to our Detroit field office for processing, so you will have about thirty minutes to think about things, before we speak again." During the remainder of the ride, all that could be heard was the SUV's contact with the pot holes in the road.

"What's to think about, I'm innocent," he said to the agent. *How the hell did they catch me? Hastings or someone else must have turned me in. But, why would Hastings have turned me in? It doesn't make any sense.*

When they arrived, Johnson was led by the two agents into an interrogation room, where they removed his handcuffs, and briefly left him. Several minutes later, agent

Miller entered and said, "I'm special agent James Miller. I'm here to take your statement." A minute later, a man opened the door and behind him Johnson could see Mohammed al-Harbia, a/k/a Hastings, being led down the hallway in handcuffs. Several seconds later, another man appeared in the doorway and closed the door behind him. Johnson thought he recognized him, but agent Miller was blocking his view. Miller looked at Johnson and said, "Say hello to my new partner, but I think you have already been introduced," he said, sarcastically.

"Hi Neal," said Frank Giordano, stepping further into the room. "I'm sorry to hear you are involved in this business. Quite frankly, I'm very surprised. If you talk to us now it will probably go better for you. Maybe they won't go for the death penalty. Just so you know we were able to trace your license plate number at Douglas Inter-State delivery, from a security camera across the street. Agent Miller's team has been following you for months. We also have you on video tape, meeting with al-Harbia in the Ford Museum. We saw him hand you the envelope full of cash. Incidentally, our investigators have determined the valve on the water heater in your mother's apartment had been tampered with. We are speculating that she was working for al-Qaeda too. Your friend, al-Harbia is probably responsible for her death.

Johnson sat there briefly, dumbfounded, angry, and speechless. *If I get a chance to be alone with Hastings, even if it's only for a few minutes, he's a dead man,* thought Johnson. After a few minutes, he said, "I'd like to speak to an attorney."